Knights of Pythias

Official Digest and Compilation of the Laws, Decisions and Enactments of the Supreme Lodge

Knights of Pythias, from its organization, August 11, 1868, to and including 1876

Knights of Pythias

Official Digest and Compilation of the Laws, Decisions and Enactments of the Supreme Lodge
Knights of Pythias, from its organization, August 11, 1868, to and including 1876

ISBN/EAN: 9783337286811

Printed in Europe, USA, Canada, Australia, Japan

Cover: Foto ©Andreas Hilbeck / pixelio.de

More available books at **www.hansebooks.com**

OFFICIAL DIGEST

AND

COMPILATION OF THE LAWS, DECISIONS AND
ENACTMENTS

OF THE

SUPREME LODGE

KNIGHTS OF PYTHIAS,

FROM ITS ORGANIZATION, AUGUST 11, 1868, TO AND IN-
CLUDING THE CENTENNIAL YEAR, 1876.

SUPPLEMENTED BY AN ANALYTICAL INDEX.

———

PREPARED BY AUTHORITY,

By F. P. DANN, P. G. C. AND P. S. R.,

SAN FRANCISCO, CAL.

———

COLUMBUS, OHIO:
PUBLISHED BY ORDER OF THE SUPREME LODGE, KNIGHTS OF PYTHIAS.
1877.

S. A. Glenn,
Printer and Electrotyper,
Columbus, Ohio.

EXPLANATORY.

At the Eighth Annual Session of the Supreme Lodge, held at the city of Philadelphia, in August, 1876, the following resolution was adopted:

Resolved, That the Digest of Laws, prepared by Representative OYLER, be referred to the Supreme Chancellor and Supreme Keeper of Records and Seal, with authority to make such additions and corrections thereto, as the legislation of this session may require, or an examination may in their judgment render proper, and with the further authority to print and promulgate the same when the finances of the Supreme Lodge justify.

Not being able to devote the time required in the preparation of an "Official Digest," we arranged with Brother F. P. DANN, P. G. C. and Supreme Representative of the Grand Jurisdiction of California, to take the work in charge. His previous experience in works of a similar character, led us to believe that he would prepare a Digest, systematic in arrangement, and complete in matter, which would meet the requirements of our Order. All documents required for the work were placed in his hands, and he has given it much time and careful preparation. We feel confident that the result of his labors will meet the hearty approval of the Lodges and members, and supply a want which has long been felt and expressed. We do not hesitate to recommend it to the Order as being practically correct, and so carefully arranged and indexed, that all can find every decision in its proper place.

We trust that every member of the Order will obtain a copy without delay, and that Lodges, Subordinate and Grand, will procure the "Official Digest" at once for the use of their officers.

Believing that the work, as prepared, will meet the approval of all,

We are, fraternally,

S. S. DAVIS,
Supreme Chancellor.

JOSEPH DOWDALL.
S. K. of R. and S.

Columbus, Ohio, July 31, 1877.

TABLE OF CONTENTS.

[The references are to pages.]

PREFACE.

At the solicitation of the Supreme Chancellor and Supreme Keeper of Records and Seal, in pursuance of the manifest desire of the Supreme Lodge, that such a work should be prepared, the undersigned has the honor of submitting to the Order the following Digest and compilation of the laws, enactments and decisions of the "Supreme Lodge, Knights of Pythias," from its organization to the present time.

In the preparation of the work, the Author has given it the most careful and thoughtful consideration, and it is believed that every enactment and decision of the Supreme Lodge, that is now law, and proper to be inserted, has been included therein.

The Certificate of Incorporation, Constitution, By-Laws and Rules of Order of the Supreme Lodge, have been inserted, immediately following the Digest, and the whole supplemented by a complete Analytical Index, alphabetically arranged in such a manner as that every subject, however incidentally referred to in any portion of the work, can be immediately found.

The various Constitutional provisions have not, as will be seen, been inserted as paragraphs in the Digest proper, such a course being deemed unnecessary, as by the Index, everything bearing upon any given subject may be easily found, and a very considerable expense in the way of printing has been thereby avoided.

The various references in connection with the Constitution, etc., will enable any one so desiring, to trace the history of every section thereof, and the reprint as notes, of the Original Constitutions, etc., which are not elsewhere to be found, will preserve those documents as so much of the history of the Order, which it is feared, will otherwise in a few years be lost to the great body of the Membership; and the numbering of the various paragraphs of the book, in connection with the Analytical Index, will materially assist in its examination.

That inaccuracies will not be found therein can hardly be expected, but hoping that they may not be many, and that such as there are, may be unimportant; and trusting that the work may prove as satisfactory to the whole Brotherhood of Knights, as the Author in its preparation has earnestly and sincerely desired that it might, it is now submitted to their honorable and candid consideration.

F. P. DANN,
P. G. C. and Supreme Representative, California.

July 2, 1877.

HISTORICAL SKETCH.

"A BRIEF SKETCH OF THE ORIGINAL HISTORY OF THE ORDER OF KNIGHTS OF PYTHIAS.

The original meeting at which the Ritual of the Order, Knights of Pythias, was first read, and the primary steps taken to establish the Order, was held in Mr. Robert A. Champion's room, 369, (old number,) F street, near the corner of Ninth street, in the City of Washington, D. C., on the evening of February 15th, 1864. There was present, on this occasion, Mr. J. H. RATHBONE, Mr. ROBERT A. CHAMPION, Mr. D. L. BURNETT, Mr. E. S. KIMBALL, Mr. W. H. BURNETT, Mr. CHAS. H. ROBERTS and Mr. DRIVER, members, (with the exception of Mr. Champion,) of a vocal society called the Arion Glee Club. At a previous meeting of the Club, Mr. Rathbone had stated to these gentlemen that he had in his possession the Ritual of a Secret Society, which he had written some time before while teaching school in the Lake Superior country, and which he was desirous of now ushering into existence. Mr. Champion, to whom Mr. Rathbone had read his Ritual, while both of them were engaged at the U. S. A. General Hospital, Germantown, Pa., in 1863, strongly urged the formation of a society, to be known as a mutual protection association among the clerks of the several Departments of the City of Washington, its members to consist of only those in clerical employment. After mutual confab on the matter, it was concluded to defer further action until the next meeting of the Club, February 15th, at which time, after the usual vocal rehearsal, Mr. Rathbone produced his ritual and a small Bible. Each of the gentlemen above named were obligated upon this Bible not to reveal that which was about to be imparted to them, and immediately afterward Mr. Rathbone began the reading of his work. After having finished the opening and closing ceremonies, Messrs. Roberts and Driver, having a previous engagement, asked to be excused, and left the room, promising, however, to abide by any action the others might take in their absence. Upon conclusion of the reading of the ritual, it was resolved that each gentleman present should consider himself a committee of one for the purpose of inviting such of his fellow clerks as he deemed would be acceptable, to join with the Club in forming the Order. At this time arrangements had just been consummated by the Club to take one of the lower rooms in the Temperance Hall Building on E street, between Ninth and Tenth, for their rehearsals, and it was resolved that if a sufficient number of members could be obtained, that the meeting should be called on the following Friday evening at this hall, the Club to call its rehearsal at 6 P. M., so as to enable the gentlemen to meet at or about 8 o'clock. At the meeting held Friday evening all present were clerks in the Departments, with the exception of Mr. Plant, who had been invited by Mr. Rathbone and Mr. Champion, on the Wednesday following the original meeting, to join the Order.

At the meeting held February 19, 1864, owing to the lateness of the hour, only the opening and closing ceremonies and the initiatory (now First) degree were read. The Second and Third degrees were left to a committee appointed by Mr. Rathbone, the W. C. of the Lodge. The committees appointed were as follows: On the Second degree, E. S. Kimball, R. A. Champion, J. T. K. Plant, W. H. Burnett and J. H. Rathbone; on the Third degree, J. R. Woodruff, D. L. Burnett and J. H. Rathbone.

The degrees, already prepared by Mr. Rathbone, were submitted to the committees, and with the exception of an addition to the Third degree, suggested by Mr. Woodruff, were approved as read, duly reported to the Lodge and adopted."—1876, *Journal*, 1272, 1277, 1279.

From the commencement the membership of the Order continued to increase, there being, however, but one Subordinate, viz: Washington Lodge. On the 8th of April, 1864, at Washington, D. C., the Grand Lodge of the District of Columbia was organized, which by virtue of its organization became the Provisional Supreme Lodge, and so continued until the formation of the Supreme Lodge as hereinafter stated.

"The Supreme Lodge, Knights of Pythias, which is the only authorized title of that body, was organized at Washington, D. C., on August 11, 1868, under and in pursuance of a "plan" which had been adopted by a Convention, held at Philadelphia, Pennsylvania, May 15, 1868, which said "plan" was, prior to the date first above mentioned, ratified by all the Grand Lodges then in existence, to-wit, of the District of Columbia, Pennsylvania, New Jersey, Maryland and Delaware.

That Convention was called agreeably to and in pursuance of Sections 1 and 2 of Article XI, of the Constitution of the Grand Lodge of the District of Columbia.

The Supreme Lodge so organized, was composed of all the Past Grand Chancellors who were then such in the various Grand Lodges above named, and in addition thereto three Representatives from each of said Grand Lodges elected for two years, at the same meeting at which the "plan" was ratified, their election as such making them Past Grand Chancellors.

By said plan all of the then officers of the said State Grand Lodges were also declared Past Grand Chancellors. The Supreme Lodge was by said plan after its organization as above, to be hailed, known and recognized as the Supreme Authority of the Knights of Pythias of the World."—1868, *Journal*, 1-15.

Exercising as it does, Executive, Legislative and Judicial functions over the whole Order, in pursuance of laws enacted for such purposes, it has continued to extend the bounds of its influence, until at this time, through varied experiences and vicissitudes, it finds itself, in less than a decade of years, exercising its influence and power over nearly one hundred thousand members, included within thirty-four Grand Jurisdictions, and twenty-six Subordinates outside of such Grand Jurisdictions.

With such a record for the early youth of the Order, what may we not expect as its years develop into a strong and sturdy manhood, and as the shadows begin to lengthen into the mellow quiet of an honorable and victorious old age?

Trusting that no stain shall ever fall upon its fair escutcheon, may we not all be permitted to express the ardent and sincere hope and wish, that its system of organized charity and benevolence may be in truth and in fact perpetual.

F. P. DANN.

OFFICIAL DIGEST.

ANNIVERSARY.

1. Day of, established.

Resolved, That the 19th day of February of each Pythian Period be, and is hereby declared to be the anniversary of the organization of the Order of Knights of Pythias.

1875, Journal, 1131, 1149.

APPEALS.

2. Certified copies of Papers necessary, etc.

Held, That certified copies of the proceedings of the Grand Lodge not having been transmitted to the Supreme Lodge, the appeal did not come up in proper form, and the papers should be returned to the Grand Lodge.

1876, Journal, 1309.

3. To be taken by Party interested. (a)

Ruled under the Constitution as then existing that only the party interested was entitled to appeal from the action of a Lodge.

1875, Journal, 1003, 1102, 1122.

4. Same.

An appeal taken by the widow of a deceased member of a Lodge, sustained by the Grand and Supreme Lodges.

1872, Journal, 551-557, 588.

5. Can only lie from action of Lodge.

An appeal does not lie from the decision of a Grand Chancellor, until the same has been acted upon by the Grand Lodge.

1875, Journal, 1102, 1131.
1874, Journal, 871, 939.
1873, Journal, 684-686, 774.

(a) The rule of this decision changed by the amendment to Article XIX, Constitution of Supreme Lodge. See Sections, 583-588.

6. Appeal Papers, by whom signed, etc.

In cases of appeal to the Supreme Lodge, the appeal papers should be signed by the Grand Chancellor and Grand Keeper of Records and Seal, with the seal of the Grand Lodge attached.

> 1875, Journal, 1103, 1132.
> 1871, Journal, 404.

7. Grand Lodge action only to be reviewed by.

A Past Grand Chancellor being deprived of his certificate by vote of his Grand Lodge, never having been instructed in the Supreme Lodge Rank, desiring to have the action of the Grand Lodge reviewed, must take an appeal to the Supreme Lodge from such action, in proper form.

> 1875, Journal, 1127, 1128, 1129.

8. Consent must be given, by whom.

Where the law required the consent of the Grand Lodge in order to authorize an appeal, such consent must come from the Grand Lodge itself, and cannot be given by the Grand Chancellor after the adjournment of the Grand Lodge.

> 1873, Journal, 703, 730-733.

9. When Papers to be sent to the Supreme Lodge, etc.

Resolved, That all appeals to the Supreme Lodge and accompanying papers shall be sent to the S. K. of R. and S., at least one month previous to the annual session of the Supreme Lodge. (a) The Supreme K. of R. and S. shall at that time place all appeals and accompanying papers in the hands of the Chairman of the Committee * * on Appeals, to enable said Committee to report fully and promptly to the Supreme Lodge at its session.

> 1872, Journal, 562, 563.

10. Irregularities, when not ground for Appeal.

The action of the Grand Lodge will not be disturbed, notwithstanding irregularities may have occurred in reaching the final result, where it appears that the final action is correct.

> 1872, Journal, 447-452, 574.

11. Judgment reversed on appeal for want of Evidence.

The Supreme Lodge reversed the judgment of a Grand Lodge by which a member was suspended, the Supreme Lodge "not finding any evidence in the case warranting suspension."

> 1870, Journal, 181, 182, 206.

(a) See as bearing on this subject Article XIX Supreme Lodge Constitution, subsequently adopted. See Sections, 583-588.

ARREARS.

12. Meaning of term, "One Year in Arrears."

The correct construction of subdivision 21 of Section 2, Article VIII, Supreme Lodge Constitution, being in the following words: "A member who is one year in arrears shall be declared suspended," is, that a member owing for twelve months' dues should be declared suspended.

1876, Journal, 1232, 1266, 1302.
1873, Journal, 705, 768.

13. Members in Arrears to be notified.

Resolved, That when a member is twelve months in arrears he should be notified thereof, and the fact of his suspension declared by the Chancellor Commander in open Lodge, and a record thereof made on the minutes.

1876, Journal, 1232, 1266, 1302.

14. When Member cannot be declared in Arrears.

A subordinate Lodge may collect dues in advance, but cannot declare a member in arrears for dues who has paid the same to the first of a term; or allow the advance payment required to invalidate the member's right to benefits or the S.A.P.W.

1875, Journal, 1042, 1097, 1114, 1121.

AYES AND NOES.

15. Calling of.

As to the calling of the ayes and noes in a Grand Lodge, it is a matter entirely local in character and under the control of the Grand Lodge itself.

1873, Journal, 703, 733.

BALLOT.

16. Who to inspect and announce.

A ballot for a candidate for membership should be inspected by the Vice Chancellor, and the result announced by the Chancellor Commander.

1876, Journal, 1227, 1266, 1296.

17. On application for Membership.

Under the present law the same ballot must be had upon an application for membership by card as by initiation.

1875, Journal, 1042, 1097, 1114, 1121.

BANNERS.

18. Design adopted.

A banner for the Order was adopted by the Supreme Lodge as follows:

DESCRIPTION OF BANNER.

"To be composed of three pieces of silk, of color and sizes as follows: Dark blue, size, 18 by 30 inches; Orange yellow, size, 18 by 30; Crimson, size, 24 by 36. Colors to be placed as per accompanying diagram. The full size of banner to be 3 by 4½ feet. Shield in center painted in white; size, 18 by 24 inches. The device on shield to be the distinction of Rank of Lodge—Supreme, Grand or Subordinate.

To Supreme Lodge—Globe, and in circle around it to be the words "Supreme Lodge of the World, Knights of Pythias."

For Grand Lodges—Grand Lodge or State Seal, and in circle around same, Grand Lodge of ...., Knights of Pythias.

To Subordinate Lodges—K. P. cut as on accompanying diagram, with name and number of Lodge, together with location; on edge of banner all around, fine gold line 1½ inches wide; on bottom, gold fringe 3 or 3½ inches deep. Staff to be of oak, or other suitable wood, 7 or 8 feet long; on top of staff, spear head; ball and falcon spear heads on ends of cross piece. All marks, devices, designs, etc., on banner to be in gold, or gold and black.

1873, Journal, 687, 688, 708, 740, 742.

BENEFITS.

19. For what, cannot be forfeited.

Membership or benefits cannot be forfeited before the time specified in the laws of the Supreme, Grand or Subordinate Lodge, by adding fines or assessments to dues.

1876, Journal, 1228, 1266, 1284, 1296, 1300.

20. What is meant by the terms "Weekly" and "Funeral" Benefits.

The "weekly" and "funeral" benefits referred to in clause 22 of Section 2, Article VIII, of the Supreme Lodge Constitution, which it is made obligatory on each Grand Lodge to require its Subordinates to provide for, contemplate such benefits as each Lodge shall provide for the payment of, out of its own funds only, and not through a combination of Lodges.

1876, Journal, 1208, 1288, 1280-1292.

21. Same.

Long usage in similar organizations, and in the Knights of Pythias, has affixed a well defined meaning to the terms "weekly" and "funeral" benefits; and in this well understood sense, the words were used in the provision of the Supreme Lodge Constitution above referred to.

1876, Journal, 1208, 1288, 1289-1292.

22. Same.

The beneficial system established by the above compulsory provision of the Supreme Lodge Constitution, excludes from the Order a beneficial system of a different kind, on the principle that the inclusion of the one system excludes the other.

1876, Journal, 1208, 1288-1292.

23. Funeral Benefits, case concerning.

The fact that a member is delinquent to his Lodge at the time of being taken sick, does not of itself exclude those entitled, from receiving funeral benefits in case of the member's death, he being square with the Lodge at the time of such death.

1876, Journal, 1318.

24. Advance Payments required, not to deprive of.

A Subordinate Lodge may collect dues in advance, but cannot declare a member in arrears for dues who has paid the same to the first of a term; or allow the advance payment required to invalidate the member's right to benefits or the S.A.P.W.

1875, Journal, 1042, 1097, 1114, 1121.

25. When to be paid sick Member leaving the country.

In the absence of any law regulating the subject, a member sick and entitled to and receiving benefits from his Lodge does not forfeit his right to continuous benefits, he still remaining sick, by leaving the country under the advice of his physician for the purpose of endeavoring to restore his health.

1875, Journal, 1102, 1147, 1148.

26. Same.

A sick brother does not forfeit his right to benefits by leaving the jurisdiction of the Relief Committee of his Lodge without their consent, or the approval of the Lodge, under a By-Law providing for such forfeiture passed subsequently to the departure of such brother.

1875, Journal, 1102, 1147, 1148.

27. Reinstated Member, when entitled to.

In the absence of any law providing otherwise, a reinstated brother becomes beneficial immediately upon his reinstatement.

1875, Journal, 1102, 1161.

28. During suspension of Lodge.

A member is not entitled to benefits during such time as his Lodge may be under suspension.

1874, Journal, 944.

29. Funeral Benefits in cases of suicide.

The granting or withholding funeral benefits to the family or near relatives of suicides within the Order, is a matter entirely of local legislation.

1873, Journal, 684, 734.

30. A fundamental Principle.

The payment of weekly and funeral benefits, is a distinguishing characteristic, and may be regarded as a fundamental principle of the Order of Knights of Pythias.

1873, Journal, 692, 693, 753.

31. Rights, not Charities.

The pecuniary benefits which the Order provides, are secured to its members as rights and not as charities, through the contribution of certain stipulated dues by all its members, at regular and established intervals of time.

1873, Journal, 692, 693, 753.

32. Subject to local Legislation.

The payment of benefits, so far as the mere amount is concerned, subject to the limit fixed by the paramount law, has always been left to local legislation.

1873, Journal, 692, 693, 753.
1872, Journal, 465, 468, 575, 612, 613, 614.

33. Funeral Benefits and Expenses.

Under the By-Laws of a Lodge which provided that "on the death of a brother, there shall be appropriated from the funds of the Lodge one hundred dollars to defray the funeral expenses," *held*, that the widow was entitled to receive any balance of said sum that might remain unexpended by said Lodge for needed funeral expenses.

1872, Journal, 551-557, 558.

34. Powers of Grand Lodge over.

It is competent for a Grand Lodge to prescribe some definite period of time within which Subordinate Lodges shall be required to pay benefits.

1872, Journal, 588, 595.

BLANKS.

35. For certain Reports provided.

By resolution of the Supreme Lodge, the following blanks are required to be furnished to each Grand Keeper of Records and Seal and Deputy Supreme Chancellor, upon which are to be reported all moneys paid by them to the Supreme Lodge. The blanks are as follows:

36.

"Office G. K. of R. and S., Grand Jurisdiction of .... No. ......

Dear Sir and Bro.:

I herewith inclose my .... for the sum of .... dollars in payment of ....

Yours fraternally,

....,
· · G. K. of R. and S.

To .... S.K. of R. and S.

37.

"Office G. K. of R. and S., Grand Jurisdiction of .... No. ......

Dear Sir and Bro.:

I have this day forwarded by .... the sum of .... dollars in payment of ....

Yours fraternally,

........................,
G. K. of R. and S.

To .... S. C.

38.

"Office G. K. of R. and S., Grand Jurisdiction of .... No. ......

Dear Sir and Bro.:

I have this day forwarded by .... the sum of .... dollars in payment of ....

Yours fraternally,

........................,
G. K. of R. and S.

To .... S. M. of E.

1873, Journal, 698, 715, 716.

CASTLE HALLS.

39. Public Dedications.

A ceremony adopted for public dedications of Castle Halls for the use of the Order, and public dedications authorized.

1871, Journal, 364, 385,
1870, Journal, 183, 188, 191, 229.

CHANCELLOR COMMANDER.

40. To announce result of Ballot.

A ballot for a candidate for membership should be inspected by the Vice Chancellor, and the result announced by the Chancellor Commander.

1876, Journal, 1227, 1266, 1296.

41. Under what circumstances may communicate S. A. P. W.

Ruled by the Supreme Chancellor, that the Chancellor Commander of a Lodge is empowered to instruct the members of his own Lodge in the Semi-Annual Pass-Word; also all members of Lodges within or without his Jurisdiction presenting an order for it, under seal of their Lodge, signed by the Chancellor Commander, attested by the Keeper of Records and Seal, and presenting the usual evidence of their good standing.

1876, Journal, 1228.

42. To have charge of Rituals.

The Rituals and other private work of the Order should be, and remain, in the charge and keeping of the Chancellor Commander of each Lodge, to be kept by him in some safe receptacle, under lock and key, within the Castle Hall of the Lodge, and not to be removed therefrom.

'1875, Journal, 1106, 1149, 1152.

43. Who eligible.

Ruled by the Supreme Chancellor, that Lodges were at liberty to elect whom they please for Chancellor Commander, if eligible otherwise under the local law. There is no general law making it rotative from lower offices up.

1872, Journal, (Appendix) 37.

44. May resign.

There is nothing in the obligation taken by the Chancellor Commander, upon his installation, that prevents him from resigning said office at any time that he may desire so to do.

1873, Journal, 564, 582, 585.

CHARGES.

45. Member refusing to receive Rank, not subject to.

Charges could not be preferred against an Esquire for refusing to proceed any farther in the Knight's Rank, after having proceeded through a portion thereof. He would not however be entitled to any benefits, privileges or honors of the Knight's Rank.

1875, Journal, 1133, 1140.

46. When holding Withdrawal Card, no bar to Charges.

A Withdrawal Card issued to a Past Chancellor by his Subordinate Lodge, while charges are pending against him in his Grand Lodge, cannot be plead in bar of the charges, but under some circumstances might be an aggravation thereof. So ruled by the Supreme Chancellor.

1873, Journal, (Appendix) 38.

47. Grand Lodge to receive and entertain.

A Grand Lodge receiving charges against one of its officers, should entertain and act upon the same, giving them a fair and proper consideration.

1871, Journal, 346, 372, 373, 392, 397-399, 405, 406, 423, 424.

CHARTER BOOKS.

48. Opening of, not allowable.

Under the existing Constitution of the Supreme Lodge, there is no such thing recognized as the opening of Charter Books, for the purpose of receiving members for a less sum than that fixed by the Constitution. That matter is regulated by Subdivision 8, Section 2, of Article VIII, of the Supreme Lodge Constitution.

1875, Journal, 1033, 1096, 1113, 1121.

CHARTERS.

49. Blank Charters.

In order to maintain uniformity, all Charter Plates are furnished as supplies by the Supreme Lodge.

1869, Journal, 68, 120.
1870, Journal, 166, 175, 214.

DEPUTY SUPREME CHANCELLOR.

50. Commission.
An official commission to be issued by the Supreme Chancellor, under his official seal, to Deputy Supreme Chancellors, was adopted by the Supreme Lodge.

> 1873, Journal, 680, 719, 746 and Appendix, 12, 13.

51. Cannot issue Dispensation for new Lodge.
A Deputy Supreme Chancellor has no authority to issue a dispensation to organize a new Lodge.

> 1868, Journal, 26, 45.

DUES.

52. All Knights must pay.
A Lodge cannot make a law exempting new members from the payment of dues for six months after being enrolled as Knights.

> 1876, Journal, 1228, 1266, 1296.

53. Non-payment of, suspends from Membership.
A member not being under charges, owing for twelve months' dues, but not less, should be declared suspended from membership.

> 1876, Journal, 1232, 1266, 1302,
> 1872, Journal, 531, 585.

54. May be collected in advance, etc.
A Subordinate Lodge may collect dues in advance, but cannot declare a member in arrears for dues, who has paid the same to the first of a term, or allow the advance payment required to invalidate the member's right to benefits or the S.A.P.W.

> 1875, Journal, 1042, 1097, 1114, 1121.

55. When may be charged against suspended Members.
Unless under the provisions of constitutional enactments, it is not lawful to charge parties suspended for non-payment of dues with dues, after the act of suspension, until reinstated.

> 1875, Journal, 1112, 1142, 1156.

56. Payment of, by Pages and Esquires.
The charging of, and collecting dues, from Pages and Esquires, is a matter entirely and solely for local legislation.

> 1873, Journal, (Appendix) 37.
> 1872, Journal, 465, 612, 613, 614.

57. Subject to local Legislation.

The fixing of the amount of dues which should be contributed by members to enable Lodges to pay sick and funeral benefits, has been left to local legislation. It is, however, the duty of all Subordinate Lodges to collect such dues from their members as may enable them to pay some such benefits.

1873, Journal, 692, 693, 753.
1872, Journal, 465, 468, 575, 612, 613, 614.

EMBLEMS.

58. Not to be displayed in business places.

Except by such parties as may be engaged in the manufacture or sale thereof, the display by members of the Order, at their places of business, of any of the emblems or insignia of the Order, or using the same in any manner as a means of advertising, is highly reprehensible; and if persisted in, the offender should be proceeded against under the law.

1875, Journal, 1133, 1144.

59. Badge adopted.

A design of badge for Past Chancellors and Knights adopted by the Supreme Lodge.

1870, Journal, 224.

60. Same.

A design for a Supreme Lodge mark or emblem was adopted.

1868, Journal, 56.

FEES.

61. To what extent obligatory.

The provision, Subdivision 8, Section 2, Article VIII, Supreme Lodge Constitution, fixing a minimum as to fees for conferring the Ranks is obligatory, and cannot be changed, except as provided in Article XXXIII of that Constitution; subject to that provision, the whole question is one for local legislation.

1876, Journal, 1230, 1286.

62. Cannot be donated to applicants for Membership.

Resolved, That the refunding, or donating, or promising, directly or indirectly, to refund or donate to applicants for membership in this Order, any portion of the initiation fee, is a violation of Section 8, of Article VIII, of the Constitution.

1875, Journal, 1133, 1140.

63. When cannot be reduced by Dispensation.

A Grand Chancellor cannot issue dispensations to initiate persons for less than the rates prescribed by law, even though he may have directions and authority from his Grand Lodge so to do.

1873, Journal, 705, 768.

FINES.

64. When Past Chancellor subject to.

Under the laws of a Lodge which provide for the fining of officers for non-attendance at meetings, the Past Chancellor necessarily becoming such by virtue of his election and service in the office of Chancellor Commander, is a sitting officer of the Lodge, and liable to fines the same as other officers.

1876, Journal, 1234, 1266, 1302, 1306.

FLAGS.

65. For Subordinate Lodge Officers.

Standards to be four feet high, three feet four inches wide, made of silk, quartite at the bottom, fastened at the top to the cross-bar by gilded spear not more than three inches in diameter; heighth of the staff to be at the pleasure of the Lodge.

66. For Prelate.

Black field, trimmed with silver fringe, with Bible in center in silver.

67. For Chancellor Commander.

Red field, trimmed with gold fringe; in center of field, a shield, battle axes, helmet and crossed gavels of gold.

68. For Vice Chancellor.

Blue field, trimmed with gold fringe; in center the coat of arms of the State (or nationality); below, a single gavel of gold circling above the name and number of the Lodge.

1872, Journal, 483, 484.
1871, Journal, 315, 341, 399.
1870, Journal, 142, 174, 192, 207, 208, 220, 221.

69. For Outside Use.

The Regulation Flag is to be six feet long and two feet six inches wide. Any other sized flag to be in width two-thirds of the length. Material to be silk, bunting or muslin. Colors, blue, yellow, and red, equal sized, vertical. Shield of Supreme Lodge, purple. "P," and Tilting Spear yellow. Shield of Grand Lodge, red. "P" and Tilting Spear yellow. Shield of Subordinate Lodge, red and white, red above. "P" and Tilting Spear yellow. The Shield, letter "P" and Spear may be painted or worked. No fringe of any kind upon this flag; the heighth of the Staff to be at the pleasure of the Lodge; Staff to be mounted with a gilded helmet head, with red cord and tassels hanging therefrom. (a)

> 1872, Journal, 483, 484.
> 1871, Journal, 315, 341, 399.
> 1870, Journal, 142, 174, 192, 207, 208, 220, 221.

FOUNDER, &c., OF THE ORDER.

70. Title of, &c.

The original title given to the Founder of the Order, by the "Plan" adopted for the organization of the Supreme Lodge, was, "Founder and Supreme Past Chancellor." This title seems however to have been transposed, from and after the organization of the Supreme Lodge, to that of, "Founder and Past Supreme Chancellor," which has been its recognized form ever since. This Rank dies with the death of JUSTUS H. RATHBONE, the Founder of the Order.

> 1868, Journal, 8, 10, 13.
> 1876, Journal, 1272, 1277–1279.

71. Regalia and Badge.

A suitable Regalia and engraved Badge, authorized to be procured for the Founder of the Order, differing from any other in the Order.

> 1868, Journal, 20, 92.
> 1876, Journal, 1282.

FUNDS.

72. Donations may be made from.

Donations from the funds of a Lodge may be made to relieve the wants of distressed brothers.

> 1876, Journal, 1308.

(a) The report of the Committee on Flag, p. 399, nowhere appears to have been adopted, although so recognized at pp. 483 and 484, Journal of 1872. The specifications, however, are believed to have been uniformly acted upon by the Order.

73. Upon what vote to be disbursed.

The funds of the Lodge, even in payment for nurse hire, cannot be disbursed upon a mere majority vote when the Laws require a two-thirds vote.

1876, Journal, 1308.

74. To aid in erection of Washington Monument.

The power of Grand and Subordinate Lodges to appropriate their funds to aid in the erection of the Washington Monument, recognized by the Supreme Lodge.

1875, Journal, 1112, 1129.

FUNERALS.

75. Regalia that may be worn at.

Lodges may appear in public parade, at funerals, wearing the funeral rosette on left breast, with or without Jewels; also in uniform, with or without Jewels, or in plain citizens' dress.

1875, Journal, 1032, 1096, 1124.

76. Rosette to be worn at Funerals by Subordinate Lodges.

At funerals, the following rosette may be worn in lieu of other regalia, viz:

77. By Knights, Pages and Esquires.

Round rosette, black, flat center, $1\frac{1}{2}$ inches in diameter, with white metal struck up or silver embroidered escutcheon, surrounded by two rows of $\frac{1}{2}$ inch black satin ribbon, the joint made by the ribbon joining the center of the rosette, to be covered with $\frac{1}{4}$ line silver braid; the completed rosette to be three inches in diameter. Suspended from the under side of the rosette a white silk ribbon $2\frac{1}{2}$ inches wide and $4\frac{1}{2}$ inches long, with name and number of Lodge, and the letters "K.P." printed upon it in black, the white ribbon to be covered with black crape.

78. By Past Chancellors.

Same as for members, but gilt escutcheon.

79. By Officers.

Same as for members, but substituting the emblem of their respective offices for the escutcheon in center of the rosette.

1872, Journal, 620, 631.
1871, Journal, 403, 413.

80. Same—by Grand Lodges.

A rosette, three inches in diameter, with black velvet center of two inches with gold letters " G. L." and one-half inch red border (ribbon.)

1869, Journal, 99, 116.

81. Order of Procession.

Resolved, That when the Order attends funerals, the line of march shall be taken up in the following order:

1st. The Outer Guard, bearing a sword, followed by the Pages, Esquires and Knights, in the order as laid down.

2d. The Inner Guard bearing a sword.

3d. Keeper of Records and Seal, Master of Finance, and Master of Exchequer (three abreast), each bearing the emblems of their respective offices.

4th. Master at Arms, bearing a staff.

5th. (a) Chancellor Commander, and Vice Chancellor, each bearing the emblems of their respective offices.

6th. (a) Past Chancellor supported by two Past Chancellors.

7th. Past Chancellors and Past Grand Chancellors.

On arriving at the grave the procession halts and opens order, when the coffin and mourners pass through, and the procession follows the corpse in a reversed position.

1871, Journal, 403, 404, 414.

82. Ritual for Funeral Services.

The Funeral Ceremony for the use of the Order adopted.

1868, Journal, 18, 19, 20, 38, 48.

GRAND CHANCELLOR.

83. What Dispensations may issue.

A Grand Chancellor may issue a dispensation to initiate a maimed person, provided he is capable of making an honest livelihood for himself and family.

1873, Journal, 710, 744, 745,
1874, Journal, 900, 932, 933,
1876, Journal, 1235, 1266, 1285, 1294.

(a) This form having been adopted before the change in officers, Nos. 5 and 6 above should be changed so as to have the Prelate accompany the Vice Chancellor, and the Past Chancellor the Chancellor Commander.

3

84. What Dispensations cannot issue.

A Grand Chancellor cannot issue dispensations to initiate persons for less than the rates prescribed by law, even though he may have directions and authority from his Grand Lodge so to do.

1873, Journal, 705, 768.

85. Filling Vacancy entitled to Honors.

A Grand Chancellor elected to fill a vacancy, who serves out the balance of the unexpired term, is entitled to the honors of the office.

1874, Journal, 899, 932, 933.

86. What cannot require.

A Grand Chancellor cannot require the Rituals of the Subordinate Lodges in his Jurisdiction, to be delivered to the Deputies after the charges are committed to memory, to be retained by such Deputies until the next installation of officers.

1873, Journal, 756.

GRAND KEEPER of RECORDS AND SEAL.

87. When to transmit Credentials.

The Grand Keepers of Records and Seal are required to transmit the credentials of Supreme Representatives and Past Grand Chancellors, at least twenty days before the session of the Supreme Lodge, to the Supreme Keeper of Records and Seal.

1871, Journal, 410.

GRAND LODGE.

88. Charter of, for what forfeited.

Any Grand or Subordinate Lodge, resorting to, instituting or promoting any scheme of raffle, lottery, gift enterprise or scheme of chance, shall forfeit its charter.

1876, Journal, 1231, 1264, 1299.

89. What Dispensations may issue.

A Grand Lodge may issue a dispensation to initiate a maimed person, provided he is capable of making an honest livelihood for himself and family.

1873, Journal, 710, 744, 745.
1874, Journal, 900, 932, 933.
1876, Journal, 1235, 1266, 1285, 1294.

90. Organization and Government of, what subject to.

All questions of the organization and government of Grand Lodges, so far as the same do not interfere with obligatory law, to be left to local legislation.

1876, Journal, 1236, 1274.
1872, Journal, 564, 594.
1870, Journal, 176, 177, 197, 200, 201, 204, 207.

91. Prohibition as to electing a Past Grand Chancellor.

Since the adoption of the Constitution of the Supreme Lodge in 1874, there has been no authority in a Grand Lodge to elect a Past Grand Chancellor from among Past Chancellors only; although there is no express, there is an implied, prohibition of such action.

1876, Journal, 1283, 1286.

92. Constitution of, by whom amended.

The power to amend the Constitution of a Grand Lodge, exists in the Grand Lodge itself, and cannot be conferred upon any other body.

1876, Journal, 1208, 1288–1292.

93. Can have but one Constitution, etc.

A Grand Lodge can have but one Constitution, which, when regularly adopted, can only be amended as therein provided; only such Constitutions or Amendments should be approved by the Supreme Lodge.

1876, Journal, 1208, 1288–1292.

94. What Jurisdiction cannot assume.

A Grand Lodge cannot, in its Constitution, assume extra territorial jurisdiction; although it is within the power of the Supreme Lodge, under the present Constitution, to place any of its Subordinates under the jurisdiction of a Grand Lodge temporarily.

1876, Journal, 1310.
1872, Journal, 620, 621, 627.

95. What should not be inserted in Constitution of.

Although it would not be illegal so to do, the provisions of the Supreme Lodge laws relative to Regalia, ought not to be introduced into a Grand Lodge Constitution, as any change made in such laws by the Supreme Lodge, would cause a conflict between the two laws.

1876, Journal, 1310.

96. Rules relative to "Uniform Divisions."

The Supreme Lodge having made no constitutional pro-vision for the organization of "Uniform Divisions," the sub-

ject matter thereof is left to the action of the several Grand
Lodges.

1876, Journal, 1303, 1315.

97. How to submit Hypothetical Questions, etc.

All hypothetical questions or propositions must be sub-
mitted to the Supreme Lodge or Supreme Chancellor, by a
Grand or Subordinate Lodge, under the jurisdiction of the
Supreme Lodge, under the seal of such Lodge.

1876, Journal, 1311.

98. How far may legislate concerning S.A.P.W.

The length of time that a member may be in arrears for
dues before he can be deprived of the S.A.P.W. is a question
subject to the legislation of State Grand Bodies, so long as
they comply with the Supreme law by suspending members
who are twelve months in arrears for dues.

1875, Journal, 1042, 1097, 1114, 1116, 1121.
1872, Journal, 466, 575, 612, 613.

99. Who eligible as Representative to.

A Chancellor Commander elected for a second term, is
entitled to the rank and title of Past Chancellor immediately after his second installation, and is thereupon eligible
to be elected as Representative to his Grand Lodge, unless
disqualified by local law.

1875, Journal, 1042, 1097, 1114, 1116, 1121.

100. To furnish Journals to Supreme Lodge.

Resolved, That all Grand Lodges are hereby ordered to
forward to the office of the S.K. of R. and S. two complete
sets of their Journals of Proceedings, and each year, or as
soon thereafter as printed, two copies of the same. All
Grand Lodges are requested to have their Journals conform
in size with Supreme Lodge Proceedings.

1875, Journal, 1106, 1124.

101. May try Officers.

As a general proposition, there are no written rules or
declaratory law for conducting proceedings upon charges
against a Grand Lodge officer. The right to try, to suspend,
or even to remove from office, do of necessity exist; and
there is no impropriety, in the absence of specific written
rules, in using as a guide, for the action of a Grand Lodge,
the laws prescribed for the government of Subordinate
Lodges in analagous cases.

1874, Journal, 861 868, 945.
1875, Journal, 1127-1129.

102. When may vacate office at Semi-Annual Session.

Under a Grand Lodge Constitution, which provided that business of a local character might be transacted at a semi-annual session, but all business of a general character affecting the interests of Subordinate Lodges throughout the State, should be transacted at the annual session; *held*, that a Grand Lodge had the right, by resolution, at a semi-annual session, to vacate the position of Grand Chancellor, and devolve the duties thereof upon the Vice Grand Chancellor, until the annual session; the laws of said Grand Lodge which might be applied to such a case, providing that an officer against whom charges are preferred, may, by resolution, vacate the position held pending trial.

1874, Journal, 861-868, 945.
1875, Journal, 1127-1129.

103. When authorized to exercise summary power.

In the occasional cases which arise, calling for the application of the principle of self-preservation, Grand Lodges have the right to deprive an officer of the exercise of official powers, by such summary methods as may be deemed necessary.

1874, Journal, 861-868, 945.
1875, Journal, 1127-1129.

104. To determine who may receive Rank of P.C.

Whether or not the Rank of Past Chancellor shall be conferred upon first K's. of R. and S., M's. of F., or M's of E., who have served a specified length of time in such positions, or upon Knights, as a reward for other meritorious services, is a matter for local Jurisdictions.

1873, Journal, 699, 703, 704, 710, 727, 732, 733, 734, 735.
1870, Journal, 185, 199.
1875, Journal, 1005, 1132, 1140, 1146, 1156.
1874, Journal, 871, 927, 940, 944.

105. Cannot install Officers by proxy.

It is contrary to the established customs and ritualistic ceremonies of the Order, to provide, that in case of the absence of an elective Grand Officer at the time of installation, he may be installed by proxy.

1875, Journal, 1139.

106. When forfeits right to Representation.

Under Articles IX and XVIII, Supreme Lodge Constitution, a Grand Lodge delinquent as therein specified, does forfeit its right to representation in the Supreme Lodge, but the Supreme Lodge may, by special vote, permit as a privilege (but not as a right) the said Grand Lodge, through its Representatives, to be heard on the floor of the Supreme Lodge.

1875, Journal, 1160, 1164.

107. Where Rank of Past Chancellor conferred.

The Past Chancellor's Rank, being a ritualistic Rank and fully provided for in the Grand Lodge Rituals, can only be conferred in the Grand Lodge, with its attendant ceremonies.

1874, Journal, 913, 935.

108. Effect of Incorporation of.

The incorporation of a Grand or Subordinate Lodge under the laws of a State, has no bearing, weight, influence or relation, save as relates to such matters as exist between them and outside parties.

1874, Journal, 934.

109. Must have Charter in Lodge Room.

A Lodge, Grand or Subordinate, has no right to work without having its Charter or Dispensation present in the Lodge or ante-room.

1872, Journal, 564, 582, 585.
1873, Journal, (Appendix) 36.

110. Institution of new Lodges.

Ruled by the Supreme Chancellor, that the method of procedure in the institution of new Lodges under the jurisdiction of a Grand Lodge, was a matter for local legislation.

1873, Journal, (Appendix), 37.

111. Right to try Members.

The Grand Lodge holds jurisdiction over its own members, and when charges are preferred against them as such, all laws operative there, or in the Subordinate Lodge, are applicable until the matter is fully determined. So ruled by the Supreme Chancellor.

1873, Journal, (Appendix), 37

112. Annulling existence of.

The right to annul the existence of a Grand Lodge cannot be exercised without the express and specific sanction of positive law. No such authority can be conferred by indirect legislation.

1873, Journal, 677–680, 682, 704, 711, 712, 713, 714,
715, 718, 719, (Appendix), 44–73.

113. Power over the subject of Benefits.

It is competent for a Grand Lodge to prescribe some definite period of time within which Subordinate Lodges shall be required to pay benefits.

1872, Journal, 588, 595.

114. Installation of Officers.

The Supreme Chancellor and Grand Chancellor being absent, held that it was entirely competent for the ceremony of installation of the officers of the Grand Lodge to be performed by a Past Grand Chancellor.

1872, Journal, 590, 591, 626.

115. Suspension of.

Under the Constitution and Laws of the Order, as then existing, the suspension of a Grand Lodge by the Supreme Chancellor, for insubordination, was confirmed by the Supreme Lodge. (a)

1873, Journal, 667, 680, 682, 713–715, (Appendix), 44-73.
1871, Journal, 262-275, 290-291, 342, 386, 387, 388, 418-421.

116. Should receive and act on Charges.

A Grand Lodge receiving charges against one of its officers, should entertain and act upon the same, giving them a fair and proper consideration.

1871, Journal, 346, 372, 373, 392, 397-399, 405, 406, 423, 424.

117. Legislation for suspension of Grand Lodges.

Occasion therefor having arisen, the Supreme Lodge adopted certain legislation providing for the suspension of insubordinate Grand Lodges, during the vacation of the Supreme Lodge, by the Supreme Chancellor and other officers. (b)

1871, Journal, 346-356, 372, 373, 392, 397-399, 418-421.

118. Officers when entitled to vote.

Unless the Constitution of a Grand Lodge otherwise provides, the elective officers are entitled to vote on all questions coming before the Grand Lodge.

1871, Journal, 361, 362, 391.

119. Time of Meeting, etc.

The determining when and how often Grand Lodges will hold their sessions, is a matter for local legislation; also when officers shall be nominated and elected.

1871, Journal, 342, 394.
1870, Journal, 176, 181, 182, 200, 201, 202.

(a) As bearing upon this question, attention is called to Sec. 6, Article VII, of the present Supreme Constitution, post 541.

(b) These rules having been applicable to a specific case, now happily ended, and not being items of general legislation, are not here inserted; but if desired, may be found at pages 419 and 420 of the Journal of 1871.

120. To furnish Constitution, etc., to Supreme Lodge.

All Grand Lodges are required to deposit with the Supreme Keeper of Records and Seal, at their own expense, one printed copy of their Constitution and By-Laws for reference by the Supreme Lodge.

1871, Journal, 426.

121. Protest should be received when respectful.

A Grand Lodge should never refuse to receive a respectful protest against its action, when presented by one or more of its officers or members.

1870, Journal, 185, 199.

122. When should not mutilate its Officers' Reports.

A Grand Lodge should not strike out any portion of a Grand Chancellor's report, against his protest or objection, when the same contains no objectionable language, nor any matter connected with the private work of the Order.

1870, Journal, 185, 199.

123. Power to assess Past Chancellors, etc.

A Grand Lodge has no power to levy assessments upon the Past Chancellors of said Grand Lodge, for the purpose of paying the expenses thereof, and thereupon refuse to admit to the Grand Lodge such as might refuse to pay the assessment.

1870, Journal, 197, 198, 203.

———

GRAND VICE CHANCELLOR.

124. Not entitled to Past Grand Chancellor's honors.

While the laws of the Order confer upon the Grand Vice Chancellor the duties and powers of Grand Chancellor, during the absence, or in case of resignation, removal or death, of the Grand Chancellor for the time being, they do not confer upon him the honors of that office.

1871, Journal, 245, 340.

125. When to perform duties of Grand Chancellor.

Under the terms of a Constitution providing, that in case of a vacancy occurring in the office of Grand Chancellor, the duties of that office shall devolve upon the Grand Vice Chancellor for the "time being," held, that a Grand Chancellor could not be elected at a special session of the Grand Lodge, but that the Grand Vice Chancellor was the only one authorized to act as Grand Chancellor, until the next regular meeting of the Grand Lodge at which officers were authorized to be elected.

1868, Journal, 26, 45.
1869, Journal, 71, 72, 86, 101, 106.

HYPOTHETICAL QUESTIONS.

126. How entertained by Supreme Lodge, etc.

Resolved, That neither the Supreme Chancellor, nor this Supreme Lodge, will hereafter receive or answer any hypothetical propositions or questions, submitted to them either in recess or during the session of the Supreme Lodge, except the same come from a Grand Lodge, or a Subordinate Lodge under the jurisdiction of this Supreme Lodge, and under the seal thereof.

1876, Journal, 1311.

127. Same.

All such matters, as specified in the last paragraph, are to be presented in proper form to the Committee on Law and Supervision, so far as possible, at least three weeks before the session of the Supreme Lodge; and all matters not presented before the assembling of the Supreme Lodge, to be thereupon presented to the Chairman of the Committee on Law and Supervision, under the penalty, if not so presented, of being subject to pass over to the subsequent session.

1873, Journal, 768.

JEWELS.

128. Lodges should procure.

For the purpose of securing uniformity, the Supreme, Grand and Subordinate Lodges should procure the Official Jewels at as early a day as possible.

1875, Journal, 1160.

129. Official and Past Official, and Knights.

By resolutions of the Supreme Lodge, "Official" and "Past Official," and "Knight's Jewels," were duly and regularly adopted, the details of which are fully presented. See post, 619–624.

1872, Journal, 562, 594, 630, 631.
1873, Journal, 692, 701, 702, 740, 742, 743, 744.
1874, Journal, 904, 905, 972–976–979, 989.
1875, Journal, 1025–1029, 1096, 1135, 1136.

130. All others illegal.

All Jewels used, worn or made by any person or persons, except as established by the above legislation, are illegal in character and unlawful in use, so far as Lodges and members of the Order of Knights of Pythias are concerned, and are prohibited from use, unless otherwise legislated by the Supreme Lodge.

1874, Journal, 972-976.

131. From whom procured.

All Jewels of the Order must be procured from the Supreme Keeper of Records and Seal, being regarded as Supplies.

1874, Journal, 972-976.

132. When may be worn in public.

The Jewels may be worn in public parades in connection with the uniform, but not otherwise.

1874, Journal, 972-976.

LAWS AND LEGISLATION.

133. Of Supreme Lodge, when binding.

Resolved, That the legislative acts of the Supreme Lodge, when they accord with the Supreme Lodge Constitution, are binding and obligatory upon Grand and Subordinate Lodges and members.

1876, Journal, 1232, 1266, 1302.

134. What repealed.

The former Constitution under which the Order had worked, and all previous legislation inconsistent with the Constitution adopted on the 25th day of April, 1874, was repealed by the Supreme Lodge on the said date.

1874, Journal, 947.

135. Curative Acts, passed by Supreme Lodge.

Legalizing the institution and work of Metropolitan Lodge, of Montreal, P. Q.

1874, Journal, 930, 931.
1875, Journal, 1035-1037, 1116, 1125.

136. Same.

Legalizing the work of the Grand and Subordinate Lodges of Pennsylvania and their officers, during the time of the troubles growing out of the promulgation of the new and Amplified Ritual.

1873, Journal, 713, 714, 715, 718, 719, 769.

137. Same.

Legalizing election of Grand Officers of Pennsylvania. The election and installation of the officers of the Grand Lodge of Pennsylvania confirmed and approved, upon their complying with the legislation of the Supreme Lodge.

1871, Journal, 428.

138. Same.

Legalizing the admission of a member under age, but the same never to be considered as a precedent for like action in the future.

1870, Journal, 140, 191, 192.

LIFE INSURANCE.

139. Compulsory Assessment for, illegal.

Resolved, That it is illegal to provide by general compulsory assessment, on all the members of the Order in a Grand Jurisdiction, for an "insurance," "relief" or "mortuary fund," in the nature of an insurance on lives.

1876, Journal, 1207, 1208, 1225, 1235, 1266, 1273,
1288, 1289–1292, 1293, 1299, 1301.
1875, Journal, 1139, 1173.

140. Foreign to the avowed purposes of the Order.

The life insurance scheme is foreign to the purposes of the Order as avowed at its origin, shown in its past history, and exemplified by the course of the Brotherhood in all Jurisdictions. And it is an innovation which might prove destructive to those purposes, being a scheme which, in a pecuniary sense, would have an overwhelming importance; so that the cultivation of Knightly friendship, the practice of the ritualistic ceremonies, and the moral teachings of the Order, which are its grand purposes, might become but mere incidents to the enforcement and development of a money-raising and money-distributing system of Life Insurance.

1876, Journal, 1208, 1288–1292.

LOCAL LEGISLATION.

141. Status of Sitting Past Chancellor, subject to.

The incidental rights, duties and responsibilities of the sitting Past Chancellor of a Lodge, are proper subjects for local legislation.

1876, Journal, 1234, 1266, 1302.
1875, Journal, 1042, 1097, 1114, 1121.

142. Organization, etc., of Grand Lodges, subject to.

All questions of the organization and government of
Grand Lodges, so far as the same do not interfere with
obligatory law, to be left to local legislation.

> 1876, Journal, 1236, 1274.
> 1872, Journal, 564, 594.
> 1870, Journal, 176, 177, 197, 200, 201, 204, 207.

**143. Semi-monthly Meetings; Reinstatement of suspended
Members, etc.**

All questions as t˅ granting Lodges the right to hold
semi-monthly meetings; also, regulating the reinstatement
o members suspended for cause; also, regulating the rights
and duties of members as between themselves, in disclosing
to each other the transactions of the Lodge; also, establishing
how many failures of Subordinates to hold regular meetings
shall forfeit charters, etc., are matters for local legislation,
and not proper subjects for determination by the Supreme
Lodge.

> 1876, Journal, 1284, 1285, 1299, 1300.

144. Fixing fees for the Ranks.

Subject to the restriction in Subdivision 8, Section 2,
Article VIII, of the Supreme Lodge Constitution, the
question as to the amount of fees that should be charged
for conferring the various ranks, is a matter entirely of
local legislation.

> 1876, Journal, 1230, 1286.

145. Rules for organization of "Uniform Divisions."

The Supreme Lodge having made no constitutional provision for the organization of "Uniform Divisions," the
subject matter thereof is left to the action of the several
Grand Lodges.

> 1876, Journal, 1303, 1315.

146. Delinquency that deprives of S.A.P.W., matter of.

The length of time that a member may be in arrears for
dues, before he can be deprived of the S.A.P.W., is a question
subject to the legislation of State Grand Bodies, so long as
they comply with the Supreme Law, by suspending members who are twelve months in arrears for dues.

> 1875, Journal, 1042, 1097, 1114, 1116, 1121.
> 1872, Journal, 466, 575, 612, 613.

147. Refusing elected Candidate admission, proper subject of.

The question of whether an elected candidate can be
refused admission to the Lodge, in case objections are found
to exist against him, and if so, what vote is requisite to
exclude him, are proper matters for local legislation.

> 1875, Journal, 1042, 1097, 1114, 1115, 1121.

148. As to charging Dues against suspended Members.

It is allowable, by local constitutional enactments, to provide for the charging of dues against members suspended for non-payment of dues, after the act of suspension, until reinstatement.

1875, Journal, 1112, 1142, 1156.

149. Rules for reinstating suspended Members.

The manner and form of, and rules for, the reinstatement of members suspended for non-payment of dues, or for other causes, are matters entirely for local legislation.

1874, Journal, 902, 909.
1871, Journal, 428.

150. Instituting new Lodges.

Ruled by the Supreme Chancellor, that the method of procedure in the institution of new Lodges, under the jurisdiction of a Grand Lodge, was a matter for local legislation.

1873, Journal, (Appendix), 37.

151. Same.

Ruled by the Supreme Chancellor, that in Jurisdictions where Grand Lodges exist, all questions as to the establishing of new Lodges in localities where a Lodge or Lodges may already exist, were matters of local legislation.

1873, Journal, (Appendix), 39.

152. Accepting rejected Applicant.

As to whether one Lodge may accept of rejected material from another Lodge, in the same locality, upon the expiration of six months' time after such rejection, is a matter for local legislation, in Jurisdictions where Grand Lodges exist. So ruled by the Supreme Chancellor.

1873, Journal, (Appendix), 39.

153. Funeral Benefits to family of Suicides.

The granting or withholding funeral benefits to the family or near relatives of suicides within the Order, is a matter entirely of local legislation.

1873, Journal, 684, 734.

154. Organizing Relief Bureaus.

The organizing and maintaining of Relief Bureaus for the care of sojourning sick members of the Order, is a matter for local legislation.

1873, Journal, 688-690, 722.
1872, Journal, 535, 536, 578.

155. Re instating suspended Members, etc.

Defining the status of suspended members, and fixing the mode and manner by which they can again be admitted to the Order, are proper matters for local legislation.

1873, Journal, 690, 734.

156. Dues and Benefits.

The regulating of dues to be collected, and benefits to be paid, within the limits established by the paramount law, has always been left to local legislation.

1873, Journal, 692, 693, 753.
1872, Journal, 465, 468, 575, 612, 613, 614.

157. Restoring surrendered Charter.

As to whether or not a surrendered Charter can be given to new petitioners, who were not members of the Lodge at its dissolution, is a proper matter for local legislation.

1873, Journal, 693, 752, 753.

158. Appointing Lecturers.

The appointing of a Lecturer, charged with the duty of visiting and instructing Lodges in the secret work, etc., is a matter for local legislation.

1873, Journal, 694, 734.

159. Conceding Rank of Past Chancellor.

Whether or not, the Rank of Past Chancellor shall be conferred upon K.'s of R. & S., M.'s of F., or M.'s of E., who have served a specified length of time in such positions, or upon any Knights as a reward for other meritorious services, is a matter for local jurisdiction.

1875, Journal, 1005, 1132, 1140, 1146, 1156.
1874, Journal, 871, 927, 940, 944.
1873, Journal, 699, 703, 704, 710, 727, 732, 733, 734, 735.
1870, Journal, 185, 199.

160. Calling of Ayes and Noes.

As to the calling of the ayes and noes in a Grand Lodge, it is a matter entirely local in character and under the control of the Grand Lodge itself.

1873, Journal, 703, 733.

161. Names on Charter.

The subject of whose names shall appear upon the Charter of a Lodge, when a Grand Lodge has been organized and the dispensation issued by the Supreme Lodge surrendered, is a matter for local legislation.

1872, Journal, 466, 575, 612, 613.

162. Levying Tax upon Members.

Whether or not, a Subordinate Lodge may levy a tax upon its members in order to enable it to meet the necessary expenses of the Lodge, is a matter purely of local legislation.

1872, Journal, 625.

163. Signing Charters.

The question as to what officers of a Grand Lodge shall sign the Charters of Subordinate Lodges under its jurisdiction, is one purely for local legislation.

1872, Journal, 377, 378, 390.

164. Fixing Time of Grand Lodge Sessions.

The determining when and how often Grand Lodges will hold their sessions, is a matter for local legislation; also, when officers shall be nominated and elected.

1871, Journal, 342, 394.
1870, Journal, 176, 181, 182, 200, 201, 202.

———

LODGE, SUBORDINATE.

165. Charter of, for what forfeited.

Any Grand or Subordinate Lodge, resorting to, instituting or promoting any scheme of raffle, lottery, gift enterprise, or scheme of chance, shall forfeit its Charter.

1876, Journal, 1231, 1264, 1299.

166. How to submit Hypothetical Questions, etc.

All hypothetical questions or propositions must be submitted to the Supreme Lodge or Supreme Chancellor, by a Grand or Subordinate Lodge under the jurisdiction of the Supreme Lodge, under the Seal of such Lodge.

1876, Journal, 1311.

167. When may refuse admission to elected Candidate.

An applicant for membership in a Subordinate Lodge under the immediate jurisdiction of the Supreme Lodge, having been elected to the Page Rank, and before being instructed in it, is found to be unworthy from facts not made known when his case was before the Lodge, may be refused admission by a majority vote of the Lodge present; and if rejected, the fee must be returned to him.

1875, Journal, 1042, 1097, 1114, 1121.

168. May collect Dues in advance, etc.

A Subordinate Lodge may collect dues in advance, but cannot declare a member in arrears for dues who has paid the same to the first of a term, or allow the advance payment required to invalidate the member's right to benefits or the S.A.P.W.

1875, Journal, 1042, 1097, 1114, 1121.

169. Upon what Terms may reinstate Members.

Lodges working directly under the control of the Supreme Lodge, may reinstate members suspended for non-payment of dues, upon the payment of one year's dues and all assessments charged during that year. Beyond this it is discretionary with the Lodge.

1875, Journal, 1043, 1097, 1114, 1121.

170. First Officers of, when acquire Past Rank.

At the institution of a Subordinate Lodge working directly under the control of the Supreme Lodge, the P.C., C.C., V.C., P., K. of R. and S., M. of F. and M. of E., take the Rank of Past Chancellor, provided said officers serve to the end of their official term. After that the Rank is obtained only by service as Chancellor Commander.

1875, Journal, 1043, 1097, 1114, 1121·

171. When may confer Esquire and Knight Ranks on Page of another Lodge.

A Subordinate Lodge may confer the Esquire and Knight Ranks on a Page who has received that Rank in another Lodge in the same or another Jurisdiction, upon a written official request of his Lodge, certifying that he has received the Rank of Page, and has paid for the other Ranks and been elected thereto. The Lodge conferring those Ranks should send to the Lodge making the request, an official notice of the Ranks having been conferred, with date ; and he should be entered on their books as holding Rank accordingly.

1875, Journal, 1043, 1097, 1114, 1121.

172. When may re-ballot upon Application for Ranks.

In Subordinate Lodges under the immediate control of the Supreme Lodge, if a Page is rejected on a ballot for the Rank of Esquire, or an Esquire on the ballot for the Rank of Knight, another ballot may be had, in either case, in one month thereafter.

1875, Journal, 1043, 1097, 1114, 1121.

173 Which Officers of, elected, and which appointed.

Under the present Constitution and Ritual of the Order, the C.C., V.C., P., K. of R. and S., M. of F. and M. of E., must be elected by ballot; the M. at A. may be elected or appointed, as each Grand Lodge may determine, and the I.G., O.G., and Attendants, must be appointed.

1875, Journal, 1043, 1097, 1114, 1121.
1873, Journal, 705, 768.

174. How Password taken up in case of Visitations.

It is competent for the Chancellor Commander of a Lodge, to appoint the Master-at-Arms to receive the Pass Word in the ante-room, from members of a visiting Lodge, after each of the visiting Knights have worked their way through the outer door, and the Lodge can then be admitted as a body.

1874, Journal, 913, 935.

175. Effect of Incorporation of.

The incorporation of a Grand or Subordinate Lodge, under the laws of a State, has no bearing, weight, influence or relation, save as relates to such matters as exist between them and outside parties.

1874, Journal, 934.

176. Who Members on Reorganization.

Upon application to reorganize a suspended Lodge, a member notified of such reorganization, and paying no attention thereto during his life, cannot be considered a member thereof at the time of his death.

1874, Journal, 944.

177. To obey Official Orders.

Ruled by the Supreme Chancellor, that a Subordinate Lodge, having received an official order from the Supreme or Grand Lodge, must act upon the same at once, prior to proceeding with any other business, and must obey such order until remedied through the proper channels.

1873, Journal, (Appendix), 35.

178. Must have Charter in Lodge Room.

A Lodge, Grand or Subordinate, has no right to work without having its Charter or Dispensation present in the Lodge or ante-room.

1872, Journal, 564, 582, 585.
1873, Journal, (Appendix), 36.

179. When may initiate Stranger of another Jurisdiction.

Lodges of one Grand Jurisdiction have no right to initiate residents of another Jurisdiction into the Order, without the consent of the Lodge nearest to which the applicant resides.

1872, Journal, 580.
1873, Journal, (Appendix), 37.

180. How to proceed at Institution of.

Ruled by the Supreme Chancellor, that at the institution of Lodges, under the control of the Supreme Lodge, the strangers must be initiated, proved and charged; the officers elected and installed; their dispensation delivered to the proper executive officer; after which they can receive applications, and perform the work usual to a Lodge, but not before.

1873, Journal, (Appendix), 37.

181. Same.

Ruled by the Supreme Chancellor, that the method of procedure in the institution of new Lodges, under the jurisdiction of a Grand Lodge, was a matter for local legislation.

1873, Journal, (Appendix), 37.

182. Subject to punishment.

Ruled by the Supreme Chancellor, that a Subordinate Lodge, issuing a Withdrawal Card to a Past Chancellor, while he was under charges in the Grand Lodge, if done through willfulness on the part of the Lodge, having full knowledge of the charges, laid itself liable to punishment by the Grand Lodge.

1873, Journal, Appendix, 37, 38.

183. Officer or Member reentering, etc.

Ruled by the Supreme Chancellor, that any officer or member retiring from the Lodge, under an order, or reentering after having performed the duty for which sent out, is not required to give the sign on retiring or returning, but must work his way through the doors.

1873, Journal, (Appendix), 38.

184. Members to be informed at the Outer Door, what Rank working in.

Ruled by the Supreme Chancellor, that it is the duty of the Outer Guard to inform a brother applying for admission, in what Rank the Lodge is working, so that errors may not occur in giving the signs, etc.

1873, Journal, (Appendix), 38.

185. How Petition endorsed.

Ruled by the Supreme Chancellor, that where no Grand Lodge exists, the petition for a new Lodge, in a locality where a Lodge already exists, should be endorsed with the approval and sanction or disapproval of the Deputy Supreme Chancellor, or officer having charge of the territory where occurring.

1873, Journal, (Appendix), 39.

186. Objections to Institution of new Lodge.

Ruled by the Supreme Chancellor, that in cases mentioned in the last paragraph, a Lodge objecting to the institution of a new Lodge in the same locality, might file its objections in writing over its seal, with the Deputy Supreme Chancellor, which should be forwarded by him to the Supreme Lodge for final passing upon the issue raised; and until so passed upon, the Deputy Supreme Chancellor should not initiate the Charter members of the new Lodge.

1873, Journal, (Appendix), 39.

187. New Lodges under jurisdiction of Grand Lodges.

Ruled by the Supreme Chancellor, that in Jurisdictions, where Grand Lodges exist, all questions as to the establishing of new Lodges, in localities where a Lodge or Lodges may already exist, were matters of local legislation.

1873, Journal, (Appendix), 39.

188. Who accepted as Charter Member.

Ruled by the Supreme Chancellor, that so long as under the control of the Supreme Lodge, no person rejected upon application to another Lodge, should be accepted on a roll of Charter members for a new Lodge. That it ought always to be made a preliminary question, "Have you ever applied to any Lodge of this Order and been rejected?" A false answer would subject the offender to punishment.

1873, Journal, (Appendix), 39.

189. When cannot accept Applicant rejected in another Lodge.

Ruled by the Supreme Chancellor, that so long as under the control of the Supreme Lodge, one Lodge cannot accept of rejected material from another Lodge in the same locality, not even after the expiration of the six months' probation required by the law, after such rejection, except by consent of the Lodge rejecting in the first instance.

1873, Journal, (Appendix), 39.

190. Same.

As to whether one Lodge may accept of rejected material from another Lodge in the same locality, upon the expiration of six months' time after such rejection, is a matter for local legislation in Jurisdictions where Grand Lodges exist. So ruled by the Supreme Chancellor.

1873, Journal, (Appendix), 39.

191. Effect of dropping Name from Petition.

The dropping of the name of an applicant for a new Lodge by ballot of the applicants, prior to the dispensation being delivered to such new Lodge, does not estop such dropped applicant from applying for membership in said Lodge, immediately after its institution, or to any other Lodge at any time; neither does such dropping constitute him a black-balled or rejected applicant, in the sense that those terms are used in the laws of the Order. So ruled by the Supreme Chancellor.

1873, Journal, (Appendix), 40.

192. Restoring surrendered Charter.

As to whether or not a surrendered Charter can be given to new petitioners, who were not members of the Lodge at its dissolution, is a proper matter for local legislation.

1873, Journal, 693, 752, 753.

193. May select its form of Ritual, when.

Subordinate Lodges have the unqualified right to select for themselves, whether they will use the Amplified Form of the Knight's Rank, or the common form, and Grand Lodges have no right or power to control them in this regard.

1873, Journal, 718.
1872, Journal, 562, 603, 609.

194. Names on Charter.

The subject of whose names shall appear upon the Charter of a Lodge, when a Grand Lodge has been organized, and the Dispensation issued by the Supreme Lodge surrendered, is a matter for local legislation.

1872, Journal, 466, 575, 612, 613.

195. Conditions on Reinstatement.

Upon the reinstatement of a Lodge, suspended for non-compliance with a law or requirement of the Supreme Lodge, proper conditions may be enforced by the Grand Lodge.

1872, Journal, 533, 567–572, 608.

196. Same.

A Lodge suspended for cause after trial, may be required, upon reinstitution thereof, to exclude all such members as were implicated in the irregularities which occasioned the suspension.

1872, Journal, 538–551, 573.

197. Suspension of Subordinate Lodge.

A Grand Lodge would be justified in suspending one of its Subordinate Lodges that should, after receiving a protest against such act, receive applications for membership from persons residing in another Jurisdiction, in a city where a Lodge existed, after being informed that such persons were residents of the foreign Jurisdiction.

1872, Journal, 538-551, 573.

198. When Charter cannot be surrendered.

Resolved, That no Subordinate Lodge shall be allowed to dissolve or surrender its Charter by vote, so long as nine (a) members remain willing to sustain the Lodge, except by permission of the Grand Lodge, or during the recess of the Grand Lodge, by the Grand Chancellor of the Jurisdiction.

1872, Journal, 563, 592, 594.

199. May appoint Chaplain.

Subordinate Lodges have the power and the right to appoint a Chaplain, to conduct the devotional exercises at funerals held under their control and direction.

1872, Journal, 563, 598.

200. How Supreme Lodge or Officers to communicate with.

The legal method of communication from the Supreme authority to the Subordinate Lodges of the several Jurisdictions, where Grand Lodges have been instituted, is through the Grand Lodges.

1872, Journal, 618, 624, 630.

201. Ruling as to Past Chancellor at Institution of Lodge. (b)

Held, by the Supreme Lodge, on inquiry by a Representative from a Grand Lodge, that in the formation of a Subordinate Lodge, the office of Past Chancellor thereof should be filled by selection of the Charter members at the institution of the Lodge, and that the person serving in that capacity until the end of the term, would have the honors of the office.

1872, Journal, 620,.630.

202. May levy Tax, when.

Whether or not a Subordinate Lodge may levy a tax upon its members, in order to enable it to meet the necessary expenses of the Lodge, is a matter purely of local legislation.

1872, Journal 625.

(a) Since the change in the law to seven members to make a Lodge, it is doubtful whether a Charter could be surrendered by vote, so long as seven even, wished to continue it.

(b) This ruling would probably be held to apply only where the local law did not otherwise provide. See post, 285.

203. Rituals not to be used in Amplified Knight's Rank.

Resolved, That the Third or Knight's Rank shall, in on instance, be conferred according to the * * Amplified Ritual of said Degree as adopted, unless the various parts have been memorized by all the persons officiating therein, so that the same can be conferred without the use of the book.

1872, Journal, 637.

204. Minors, Ladies, and Colored Persons.

The Supreme Lodge does not recognize Lodges of the Knights composed of ladies, minors or colored persons.

1871, Journal, 260, 313, 315, 341, 379, 382, 383.
1872, Journal, 564, 599.
1869, Journal, 68, 86, 96, 101.

205. Signing Charters.

The questi n as to what officers of a Grand Lodge shall sign the Charters of Subordinate Lodges under its jurisdiction, is one purely for local legislation.

1872, Journal, 377, 378, 390.

206. As to Card of Charter Member of New Lodge.

Any member of the Order desiring to assist in the formation of a new Lodge, and signing an application for such purpose, must, upon the institution of such Lodge, present his Withdrawal Card from his Lodge.

1870, Journal, 225.

207. Vouching in Lodges.

No vouching is allowed in the Order under any circumstances.

1870, Journal, 144, 229.

208. Ante-room, condition of, on opening Lodge.

No person but the Outer Guard is allowed in the ante-room at the opening of a Lodge.

1870, Journal, 229.

209. Naming Lodges.

All State Jurisdictions are prohibited from accepting the name of any living person as the name of a Lodge in their respective Jurisdictions.

1869, Journal, 85, 95.

210. Constitutions, by whom framed.

State Grand Lodges are authorized to adopt Constitutions for the government of Subordinate Lodges, provided the same do not conflict with the laws of general application ;

and provided further, that the obligatory rules and principles contained in Article VIII, of the Supreme Lodge Constitution, are incorporated therein.

Constitution of Supreme Lodge, Article VIII.
1869, Journal, 67, 88, 115.

MANUAL OF TACTICS.

211. Ruling concerning.

The Supreme Lodge having adopted a " Manual of Tactics," no other can be used. So ruled by the Supreme Chancellor.

1875, Journal, 1041, 1097, 1114, 1115, 1121.

212. Declaration concerning.

The Supreme Lodge declared that the Manual of Tactics, already approved and adopted, was ample in form, effective in its system, and adapted to the quasi-military wants of the Order.

1873, Journal, 696, 697, 737.

213. Adopted by Supreme Lodge.

A Manual of Tactics was adopted by the Supreme Lodge for the use of the Order, embracing all essential instruction from the school of the Knight to that of the Battalion.

1872, Journal, 531, 602.

MEMBERSHIP.

214. Who to inspect Ballot on application for.

A ballot for a candidate for membership should be inspected by the Vice Chancellor, and the result announced by the Chancellor Commander.

1876, Journal, 1227, 1266, 1296.

215 When Member holding Withdrawal Card, may apply for.

A member holding a Withdrawal Card in force, applying to a Lodge for membership by deposit of same, and being rejected, may apply again to any other Lodge; or, in the absence of any local law, to the same Lodge at any time.

1876, Journal, 1228, 1266, 1296.

216. For what cannot be forfeited

Membership or benefits cannot be forfeited before the time specified in the laws of the Supreme, Grand or Subordinate Lodge, by adding fines or assessments to dues.

1876, Journal, 1228, 1266, 1284, 1296, 1300.

217. Non-payment of Dues suspends from.

A member not being under charges, owing for twelve months' dues, but not less, should be declared suspended from membership.

> 1876, Journal, 1232, 1266, 1302.
> 1872, Journal, 531, 585.

218. Suspension from, to be declared, etc.

Resolved, That when a member is twelve months in arrears, he should be notified thereof, and the fact of his suspension declared by the Chancellor Commander, in open Lodge, and a record thereof made on the minutes.

> 1876, Journal, 1232, 1266, 1302.

219. Suspension from, for what.

Any individual member of any Lodge, who shall resort to, institute or promote any scheme of raffle, lottery, gift enterprise, or scheme of chance of any kind, shall be suspended from the Order.

> 1876, Journal, 1231, 1264, 1299.

220. How Maimed Person made eligible to.

Resolved, That this Supreme Lodge hereby authorizes any Grand Lodge, in open session, to grant a dispensation to any of its Subordinates to initiate a maimed person into the Order; provided, that in no instance shall a dispensation be granted to a person, incapable of making a honest livelihood for himself and family.

> 1873. Journal, 710, 720, 744, 745.
> 1874, Journal, 900, 932, 933.

221. Same.

The discretion allowed to Grand Lodges, when in session, by the above resolution, is extended to Grand Chancellors, during the recess of the Grand Lodge.

> 1876, Journal, 1235, 1266, 1285, 1294.

222. Same.

Upon application from a Subordinate Lodge, under the immediate jurisdiction of the Supreme Lodge, under its Seal, approved by the Deputy Supreme Chancellor of the District or Jurisdiction, the Supreme Chancellor may grant a dispensation for the admission of a maimed person, if in his judgment it appears proper, subject to the same restrictions made to Grand Lodges as above stated.

> 1875, Journal, 1040, 1097, 1114, 1121.

223. As to suspension of Maimed Members.

Resolved, That the laws of this Order do not require the suspension of a member who, after his initiation, has been maimed.

1873, Journal, 744, 745, (Appendix), 33, 34.
1874, Journal, 932, 933.

224. Acquired by Deposit of Certificate under Seal, upheld.

A member having been voted a Withdrawal Card by his Lodge, received in place thereof—the Lodge having no Cards —a Certificate under the Seal of the Lodge. This was accepted by the Grand Chancellor upon application for a Charter for a new Lodge; the member was elected to the office of Chancellor Commander of the new Lodge, and served in that capacity, bearing his portion of the Lodge's burdens. No charges being preferred against him, and all having acted in the matter in good faith : *held*, that he was entitled to his membership in the new Lodge, and to his honors as Past Chancellor thereof.

1876, Journal, 1305, 1306.

225. Hawaiians not eligible to.

The aboriginal natives of the Hawaiian or Sandwich Islands, are not eligible to membership in the Order under the Constitution and Laws as at present existing.

1875, Journal, 1037, 1096, 1099, 1129, 1130.

226. Elected Candidate may be refused Admission, when.

An applicant for membership in a Subordinate Lodge, under the immediate jurisdiction of the Supreme Lodge, having been elected to the Page Rank, and before being instructed in it, is found to be unworthy from facts not made known when his case was before the Lodge, may be refused admission by a majority vote of the Lodge present, and if rejected the fee must be returned to him.

1875, Journal, 1042, 1097, 1114, 1121.

227. Same.

The question of whether an elected candidate can be refused admission to the Lodge in case objections are found to exist against him, and if so, what vote is requisite to exclude him, are proper matters for local legislation.

1875, Journal, 1042, 1097, 1114, 1115, 1121.

228. Ballot upon Application for.

Under the present law the same ballot must be had upon an application for membership by card as by initiation.

1875, Journal, 1042, 1097, 1114, 1121.

229. How Member reinstated to, in certain cases.

Lodges working directly under the control of the Supreme
Lodge, may reinstate members suspended for non-payment
of dues, upon the payment of one year's dues and all assessments charged during that year. Beyond this it is discretionary with the Lodge.

1875, Journal, 1043, 1097, 1114, 1121.

230 Ruling as to suspended Members being subject to Dues.

Unless under the provisions of constitutional enactments,
it is not lawful to charge parties, suspended for non-payment
of dues, with dues, after the act of suspension, until reinstated.

1875, Journal, 1112, 1142, 1156.

231. Applicants for, cannot be donated Fees.

Resolved, That the refunding, or donating, or promising
directly or indirectly, to refund or donate to applicants for
membership in this Order, any portion of the initiation
fee, is a violation of Section 8 of Article VIII, of the Constitution.

1875, Journal, 1133, 1140.

232. Reinstatement to, a local matter.

The manner and form of, and rules for the reinstatement
of members suspended for non-payment of dues, or for other
causes, are matters entirely for local legislation.

1874, Journal, 902, 909.
1871, Journal, 428.

233. When not continued on reorganization of Lodge.

Upon application to reorganize a suspended Lodge, a
member notified of such reorganization, and paying no
attention thereto during his life, cannot be considered a
member thereof at the time of his death.

1874, Journal, 944.

234. When may be acquired out of jurisdiction of Residence.

Lodges of one Grand Jurisdiction have no right to initiate residents of another Jurisdiction into the Order, without the consent of the Lodge nearest to which the applicant resides.

1872, Journal, 580.
1873, Journal, (Appendix), 37.

235. Can only be in one Lodge.

Ruled by the Supreme Chancellor, that a person cannot
be a member of two Subordinate Lodges of the Order at the
same time.

1873, Journal, (Appendix), 37.

236. Withdrawing Application for.

An application for membership cannot be withdrawn, even by unanimous consent, after the report of the Committee of Investigation has been read to the Lodge. So ruled by the Supreme Chancellor.

1873, Journal, (Appendix), 38.

237. Ballot on Application for.

Ruled by the Supreme Chancellor, that three black balls appearing on the first ballot, the applicant for membership is rejected, and no other ballot is required to be taken.

1873, Journal, (Appendix), 39.

238. Soliciting Candidates to join the Order.

Great caution and discrimination should be used in the solicitation of candidates for membership in the Order, although the Supreme Lodge refused to declare such practice wrong or to forbid it.

1871, Journal, 401, 413.

239. Persons unable to Write not eligible.

Persons who are unable to write are not eligible for membership in the Order. A person admitted as a Page, who is able to write his name, is entitled to advance in the Order.

1873, Journal, 687, 768.
1870, Journal, 177, 204, 229.

240. Reinstating suspended Members etc.

Defining the status of suspended members, and fixing the mode and manner by which they can again be admitted to the Order, are proper matters for local legislation.

1873, Journal, 690, 734.

241. Reinstatement of suspended Members.

Under the By-Laws of a Lodge, providing that "a brother suspended for non-payment of dues shall be reinstated by paying up all arrearages," *held*, that upon such payment, the brother was thereby reinstated, without any written application to the Lodge, or further action on his part.

1872, Journal, 566, 567, 588, 589.

242. Colored Persons, Ladies and Minors.

Ladies, minors and colored persons, are not eligible to membership in the Order.

1872, Journal, 564, 599.
1871, Journal, 260, 313, 315, 341, 379, 382, 383.
1869, Journal, 68, 86, 96, 101.

243. Reinstatement by order of Supreme Lodge.

All Subordinate Lodges having suspended any member or members, for subscribing to the obligation issued by the Supreme Lodge, relative to the S.P.K., are directed forthwith to reinstate such member or members to their full rights of membership, and to refrain from enforcing from such members the payment of any dues or penalties during the continuance of such suspension. The above requirement to be carried into effect by the several Grand Lodges.

1871, Journal, 427.

244. Effect of Suspension for Non-payment of Dues.

A brother suspended for non-payment of dues, ceases to be a member of the Order until he is reinstated.

1870, Journal, 225.

MEMORIAL CHART.

245. To be furnished as other Supplies.

Resolved, That the Official Memorial Chart and Patent of Membership, shall hereafter be furnished by the Supreme Keeper of Records and Seal, to the Grand Keepers of Records and Seal, and through them to the several Subordinate Lodges, in the same manner as all other Supplies.

1875, Journal, 1155.

246. Official Memorial Charts adopted.

By resolutions of the Supreme Lodge, an "Official Memorial Membership Chart and Patent of the Order," was duly and regularly adopted, the details of which are fully presented.

1874, Journal, 904, 979–983, 989.
1875, Journal, 1022–1024, 1096, 1126.

247. Same. Official Recognition of all other Charts withdrawn.

The Supreme Lodge, by resolution, withdrew, rescinded and annulled, all official recognition heretofore given to any Chart, by whomsoever issued, and requested the various Grand Lodges to order their Subordinates hereafter to attach their seals to none other than the said Official Memorial Chart.

1874, Journal, 904, 979-983.

NAME OF ORDER.

248. Use of Name for Advertising.

No member of the Order has the right to make use of the name of the Order publicly, in any manner, for pecuniary benefit, except in advertising periodicals, supplies or regalia for the Order.

1870, Journal, 188, 209, 229.

OFFENCES.

249. Promoting Raffles, Lotteries, etc.

Resolved, That no Grand Lodge, nor Subordinate Lodge of this Order, nor any individual member of any Lodge, shall, in the name of the Order, resort to, institute or promote, any scheme of raffle, lotteries, gift enterprises, or schemes of chance of any kind. Any Grand Lodge violating this rule, shall forfeit its Charter to the Supreme Lodge. Any Subordinate Lodge violating this rule, shall forfeit its Charter to its Grand Lodge. Any individual member of any Lodge who shall violate this rule, shall be suspended from the Order.

1876, Journal, 1231, 1264, 1299.

250. Using the Emblems, etc., of the Order, for Advertising, etc.

Except by such parties as may be engaged in the manufacture or sale thereof, the display by members of the Order, at their place of business, of any of the emblems or insignia of the Order, or using the same in any manner as a means of advertising, is highly reprehensible, and if persisted in, the offender should be proceeded against under the law.

1875, Journal, 1133, 1143.

251. Using Name of the Order.

No member of the Order has the right to make use of the name of the Order publicly, in any manner, for pecuniary benefit, except in advertising periodicals, supplies or regalia for the Order.

1870, Journal, 188, 209, 229.

252. Criminal Intent an Element in every Offence.

Where no criminal intent appeared, the judgment of a Lodge, finding a member guilty of an offence, was reversed.

1874, Journal, 871, 938.

OFFICE.

253. When may be vacated. Special Case.

Under a Grand Lodge Constitution, which provided that business of a local character might be transacted at a semi-annual session, but all business of a general character, affecting the interests of Subordinate Lodges throughout the State, should be transacted at the annual session: *held*, that a Grand Lodge had the right, by resolution, at a semi-annual sesion, to vacate the position of Grand Chancellor, and devolve the duties thereof upon the Grand Vice Chancellor, until the annual session; the laws of said Grand Lodge which might be applied to such a case, providing that an officer, against whom charges are preferred, may, by resolution, vacate the position held, pending trial.

1874, Journal, 861-868, 945.
1875, Journal, 1127-1129.

254. Honors of Office.

The honors of the same office can be given to but one person for the same term.

1872, Journal, 564, 582, 585.

255. Grand Vice Chancellor, Honors of.

While the laws of the Order confer upon the Grand Vice Chancellor the duties and powers of the Grand Chancellor, during the absence, or in case of resignation, removal or death of the Grand Chancellor, for the time being, they do not confer upon him the honors of that office.

1871, Journal, 245, 340.

OFFICERS.

256. Which elected and which appointed.

Under the present Constitution and Ritual of the Order, the C.C., V.C., P., K. of R. and S., M. of F., and M. of E., must be elected by ballot; the M. at A. may be elected or appointed as each Grand Lodge may determine; and the I.G., O.G., and Attendants must be appointed.

1875, Journal, 1043, 1097, 1114, 1121.
1873, Journal, 705, 768.

257. When first Officers acquire Past Rank.

At the institution of a Subordinate Lodge, working directly under the control of the Supreme Lodge, the P.C., C.C., V.C., P., K. of R. and S., M. of F., and M. of E., take the Rank of Past Chancellor, provided said officers serve to the end of their official term.   After that the Rank is obtained only by service as Chancellor Commander.

1875, Journal, 1043, 1097, 1114, 1121.

258. Of Grand Lodges, subject to Trial.

As a general proposition, there are no written rules or declaratory law for conducting proceedings upon charges against a Grand Lodge officer. The right to try, to suspend, or even to remove from office, do of necessity exist, and there is no impropriety, in the absence of specific written rules, in using, as a guide for the action of a Grand Lodge, the laws prescribed for the government of Subordinate Lodges in analagous cases.

1874, Journal, 861–868, 945.
1875, Journal, 1127–1129.

259. When may be nominated.

Under Subdivision 5, of Section 2, Article VIII, Supreme Lodge Constitution, independent nominations for the officers of a Subordinate Lodge may be made upon the night of election, as also on the night of meeting preceding.

1875, Journal, 1131, 1139, 1140.

260. Cannot be installed by Proxy.

It is contrary to the established customs and ritualistic ceremonies of the Order, to provide, that in case of the absence of an elective Grand Officer, at the time of installation, he may be installed by proxy.

1875, Journal, 1139.

261. When need not give Sign on entering, etc.

Ruled by the Supreme Chancellor, that any officer or member retiring from the Lodge under an order, or reentering after having performed the duty for which sent out, is not required to give the sign in retiring or returning, but must work his way through the doors.

1873, Journal, (Appendix), 38.

262. Installation of Grand Lodge Officers.

The Supreme Chancellor and Grand Chancellor being absent, *held*, that it was entirely competent for the ceremony of installation of the officers of the Grand Lodge to be performed by a Past Grand Chancellor.

1872, Journal, 590, 591, 626.

263. Of Grand Lodge, when entitled to vote.

Unless the Constitution of a Grand Lodge otherwise provides, the elective officers are entitled to vote on all questions coming before the Grand Lodge.

1871, Journal, 361, 362, 391.

263a. Must not exceed Instructions.

Officers or Trustees of a Lodge should be governed by, and not exceed, any instructions they may receive from their Lodge.

1871, Journal, 374 376, 395.

263b. Election of.

Ruled by the Supreme Lodge, that although Supreme Lodge Officers were required to be elected by ballot, still it was competent, in cases where there was but one nominee for an office, to authorize by motion, one member to cast the vote of the Supreme Lodge for such nominee.

1870, Journal, 194, 195, 196.

263c. Same.

Notwithstanding such motion, however, it is still the right of every member of the Supreme Lodge present, to vote for such officer, if he desires so to do.

1870, Journal, 194, 195, 196.

263d. Resolution as to Mileage.

No Supreme Lodge Officer or Representative shall receive his mileage and expenses, unless he is present at the close of the session, or is excused by the Supreme Chancellor.

1869, Journal, 94.

OFFICIAL ORGAN.

264. Of Supreme Lodge.

The Supreme Lodge, while encouraging all reputable publications in the interest of the Order, does not recognize any publication, of whatever name, as its official organ.

1873, Journal, 710, 721.

OFFICIAL RECEIPT.

265. Should always accompany Order for S.A.P.W.

A Chancellor Commander may require a visiting brother presenting an order for the semi-annual pass word, to show a receipt for dues before instructing him in the word. A receipt should always accompany an order for the semi-annual password. Only the Official Receipt can be recognized as legal.

1876, Journal, 1227, 1266, 1206.

266. Resolutions establishing.

Resolved, That the Supreme Chancellor and the Supreme Keeper of Records and Seal be, and hereby are authorized to issue receipts, which shall be furnished to all Grand and Subordinate Lodges at $2.00 per 100; and that no receipt shall be authoritative or evidence of payment of dues, assessments or other claims of the Lodge, unless written upon such receipt, and bearing the seal of the Supreme Lodge.

Resolved, That the receipt above mentioned, go into effect on and after July 1st, 1875.

1875, Journal, 1165.

267. Form of Receipt.

(FRONT.)

OFFICIAL RECEIPT FOR DUES—Not genuine unless bearing on its back the Seal of the Supreme Lodge and the signature of the Supreme Keeper of Records and Seal.

No. _____ .... LODGE, No. _____ , K. OF P.

.................................., _____ 187 ____ .

Received of Brother ....

Dues from _____ 187 ____ *to* _____ 187 ____ $ _____

Assessments ....

Widows' and Orphans' Fund ....

Other Claims ....

$ _____

Impress Lodge Seal on this Receipt. *Master of Finance.*

(BACK.)

Office of the SUPREME KEEPER OF RECORDS & SEAL,

Columbus, Ohio, June 24, 1875, Pythian Period XII.

At the Seventh Annual Session of the Supreme Lodge Knights of Pythias of the World, held in the City of Washington, Grand Jurisdiction of the District of Columbia, May 18, 19, 20, 21 and 22, 1875, the following was adopted :

"WHEREAS, Much trouble and difficulty has from time to time occurred from the want of an authoritative receipt, which shall, upon its face not only show the payment of all claims of the Lodge against a Brother, but also be authoritative evidence to the Order throughout the World, not only of membership, but good standing in the Order ; therefore be it

"*Resolved*, That the Supreme Chancellor and Supreme Keeper of Records and Seal be, and hereby are authorized to issue receipts, which shall be furnished to all Grand and Subordinate Lodges at $2.00 per 100 ; and that no receipt shall be authoritative or evidence of payment of dues, assessments, or other claims of a Lodge against a member of a Subordinate Lodge unless written upon such receipt, and bearing the Seal of the Supreme Lodge.

"*Resolved*, That the receipt above mentioned go into effect on and after July 1st, 1875." JOSEPH DOWDALL, *Supreme Keeper of Records and Seal.*

[SEAL OF SUPREME LODGE.]

268. Effect of.

The Official Receipt is authoritative evidence to the Order throughout the World, not only of membership but of good standing in the Order.

1875, Journal, 1165.

PAGE, ESQUIRE AND KNIGHT.

268a. Withdrawal Card to issue to, when.

A Page, having become such in a Lodge that thereafter becomes extinct, wishing to connect himself with the Order in another Jurisdiction, would be entitled to a Card issued from the Grand Lodge, under the jurisdiction of which he was a member, which he would be entitled to deposit in another Jurisdiction, as in other cases.

1876, Journal, 1311, 1314.

268b. When entitled to visit Lodge.

Ruled by the Supreme Chancellor, that Pages and Esquires are entitled to be admitted into a Lodge, when opened and working in those Ranks respectively, and if having to pass the outer door, they should do so upon the order of the Chancellor Commander.

1873, Journal, (Appendix), 38.

268c. Semi-Annual Password not given to.

Ruled by the Supreme Chancellor, that Pages and Esquires cannot be invested with the Semi-annual Password.

1873, Journal, (Appendix), 38.

268d. "Sir" not used.

The word "Sir" should not be used in designating members of the Knight Rank in the Order.

1872, Journal, 563, 564 598.

268e. Terms applicable to Esquire and Knight Ranks.

The terms "prove" and "charge" and their derivatives applied respectively to the conferring of the Esquire and Knight Ranks.

1871, Journal, 364, 365, 385.

PASSWORDS.

269. Receipt for Dues to accompany Order for Password.

A Chancellor Commander may require a visiting brother, presenting an order for the Semi-annual Password, to show a receipt for dues before instructing him in the word.   A receipt should always accompany an order for the Semi-annual Password. Only the Official Receipt can be recognized as legal.

1876, Journal, 1227, 1266, 1296.

270. When Chancellor Commander may instruct in.

Ruled by the Supreme Chancellor, that the Chancellor Commander of a Lodge is empowered to instruct the members of his own Lodge in the Semi-annual Password; also, all members of Lodges within or without his Jurisdiction, presenting an order for it, under Seal of their Lodge, signed by the Chancellor Commander, attested by the Keeper of Records and Seal, and presenting the usual evidence of their good standing.

1876, Journal, 1228.

271. Semi-Annual, issued by Supreme Chancellor.

The Supreme Chancellor is authorized to issue a Universal Semi-annual Password, which, in connection with the usual evidence of good standing, shall be sufficient to admit any brother into any Lodge of the Order.

1875, Journal, 1103, 1106, 1144–1146.
1868, Journal, 18, 55.

272. When Member entitled to Semi-Annual.

A member, to be entitled to the Semi-annual Password, must pay all dues to the commencement of a term. This is, however, subject to the right of State Grand Bodies to determine the length of time a member may be in arrears, before he can be deprived of such password.

1875, Journal, 1042, 1097, 1114, 1116, 1121.
1872, Journal, 466, 575, 612, 613.

273. Supreme Chancellor may rescind.

The Supreme Chancellor is authorized to rescind the Semi-annual Password of a Grand Jurisdiction, providing the exigencies of the case demand it.

1875, Journal, 1115, 1116.

274. Advance payments required not to deprive of S.A.P.W.

A Subordinate Lodge may collect dues in advance, but cannot declare a member in arrears for dues, who has paid the same to the first of a term; or allow the advance payment required, to invalidate the member's right to benefits or the S.A.P.W.

1875, Journal, 1042, 1097, 1114, 1121.

275. How may be taken up, upon Lodge Visitation.

It is competent for the Chancellor Commander of a Lodge to appoint the Master at Arms, to receive the Password in

the ante-room, from members of a visiting Lodge after each
of the visiting Knights have worked their way through the
outer door, and the Lodge can then be admitted as a body.

1874, Journal, v13, 935.

276. As to Member holding Withdrawal Card being entitled to P.W.

Ruled by the Supreme Chancellor, that a member holding
a Withdrawal Card, was entitled to the Semi-annual Password for the term in which issued, and inferentially to visit
Lodges on such Password during such term.

1873, Journal, (Appendix), 36.
1872, Journal, 467, 575, 612, 613.

277. Semi-Annual, in what Rank used.

The Semi-Annual Password can only be used, given or
taken, in connection with, and for the purpose of determining a member's right to sit in the Lodge when open in the
Knight's Rank.   So ruled by the Supreme Chancellor.

1873, Journal, (Appendix), 38.

278. When Chancellor Commander may exact.

Ruled by the Supreme Chancellor, that the Chancellor
Commander of a Lodge has the right to exact the Semi-
Annual Password, whenever, and wherever, he deems the
safety of the work requires it, or whenever any doubt exists
as to a person's good standing or right to attend the Lodge.

1873, Journal, (Appendix), 38.

279. Persons not in possession of, when to be excluded.

A Subordinate Lodge has the right, and it is its duty, to
refuse admission to any one unless in possession of the
S. A. P. W., as also the ante-rooms must be cleared of all
who are without it, be they members or candidates, unless
otherwise ordered by the Chancellor Commander.   So ruled
by the Supreme Chancellor.

1873, Journal, (Appendix), 38.

280. May be communicated to C. C. outside of Lodge Room.

The Grand Chancellor, or his Deputy, may instruct the
Chancellor Commander in the Semi-annual Password, outside of the Lodge Room.

1873, Journal, 703, 723, 724.

281. To whom P.W. given.

The Term Password is to be communicated to Knights
only ; it cannot be given to Pages or Esquires.

1870, Journal, 229.
1873, Journal, (Appendix), 38.

282. Grand Lodge Password.

The Password of the Grand Lodge is changed annually, and is uniform throughout the Order, and to emanate from the Supreme Lodge, through the Supreme Chancellor.

1869, Journal, 67, 101.

———

PAST CHANCELLOR.

283. Who eligible to election to office of.

No one but a Past Chancellor can be directly elected to fill the office of Past Chancellor in a Lodge, in case of a vacancy, for any cause, occurring in the said position.

1876, Journal, 1234, 1266, 1302.

284. When Member filling office of, subject to fine.

Under the laws of a Lodge which provide for the fining of officers for non-attendance at meetings, the Past Chancellor necessarily becoming such by virtue of his election and service in the office of Chancellor Commander, is a sitting officer of the Lodge, and liable to fines the same as other officers.

1876, Journal, 1234, 1266, 1302, 1306.

285. Rights, Duties and Responsibilities of, what subject to.

The incidental rights, duties and responsibilities of the sitting Past Chancellor of a Lodge, are proper subjects for local legislation.

1876, Journal, 1234, 1266, 1302.
1875, Journal, 1042, 1097, 1114, 1121.

286. When reelected Chancellor Commander entitled to Rank of.

A Chancellor Commander elected for a second term, is entitled to the Rank and title of Past Chancellor, and to wear the Regalia of that Rank immediately after his second installation, and is thereupon eligible to be elected as Representative to his Grand Lodge, unless disqualified by local law.

1875, Journal, 1042, 1097, 1114, 1121.
1872, Journal, 468, 575, 613.

287. When First Officers of Lodge acquire Rank of.

At the institution of a Subordinate Lodge, working directly under the control of the Supreme Lodge, the P.C., C.C., V.C., P., K. of R. and S., M. of F., and M. of E., take the Rank of Past Chancellor, provided said officers serve to the end of their official term. After that the Rank is obtained only by service as Chancellor Commander.

1875, Journal, 1043, 1097, 1114, 1121.

288. Same.

Held, by the Supreme Lodge, on inquiry by a Representative from a Grand Lodge, that in the formation of a Subordinate Lodge, the office of Past Chancellor thereof should be filled by selection of the Charter members at the institution of the Lodge, and that the person serving in that capacity until the end of the term, would have the honors of the office.

1872, Journal, 620, 630.

289. Sitting P.C. taking Card, what Rank.

If a sitting Past Chancellor takes a · Withdrawal Card from his Lodge, upon depositing the same in another Lodge, he would take the Rank of Past Chancellor. A Rank Credential as Past Chancellor should also be issued to him with the Card, upon which he would be entitled to receive the Grand Lodge Rank.

1875, Journal, 1043, 1097, 1114, 1121.

290. Conferring Rank of, matter for Local Jurisdictions.

Whether or not the Rank of Past Chancellor shall be conferred upon K's of R. and S., M's of F.. or M's of E., who have served a specified length of time in such positions, or upon any Knights, as a reward for other meritorious services, is a matter for local Jurisdictions.

1875, Journal, 1005, 1132, 1140, 1146, 1156.
1874, Journal, 871, 927, 940, 944.
1873, Journal, 699, 703, 704, 710, 727, 732, 733, 734, 735.
1870, Journal, 185, 199.

291. Where Rank conferred.

The Past Chancellor's Rank, being a Ritualistic Rank, and fully provided for in the Grand Lodge Rituals, can only be conferred in the Grand Lodge, with its attendant ceremonies.

1874, Journal, 913, 935.

292. Rank Credentials of.

Ruled by the Supreme Chancellor, that the Past Official Rank of Past Chancellor or Past Grand Chancellor, must be evidenced by a certificate, signed by the proper Grand Officers, duly attested with the Grand Lodge Seal, prior to said Official Rank being recognized, when affiliating by Card in any other Lodge than the one in which being a member, where said Rank was attained.(a)

18'3, Journal, (Appendix), 36.

(a) See as bearing upon this subject post, 305, 461, 463, and Article XXIV, Supreme Lodge Constitution.

293. Past Chancellor in full.

A Past Chancellor in full, is one who has been regularly obligated and instructed, in the Grand Lodge, in that Rank.

1873, Journal, 568, 575, 613.

294. Past Rank under Provisional Supreme Lodge.

Ruled by the Supreme Lodge, that under the Laws of the Provisional Supreme Lodge, the Recording Scribes and Bankers, serving in such offices for one year, or filling the unexpired part of a term, were entitled to the Rank of Past Chancellor.

1869, Journal, 87, 106.
1870, Journal, 186, 225, 226.

295. Taxation of, by Grand Lodge.

A Grand Lodge has no power to levy assessments upon the Past Chancellors of said Grand Lodge, for the purpose of paying the expenses thereof, and thereupon refuse to admit to the Grand Lodge such as might refuse to pay the assessment.

1870, Journal, 197, 198, 203.

PAST GRAND CHANCELLOR.

296. Who not eligible to election as.

Since the adoption of the Constitution of the Supreme Lodge, in 1874, there has been no authority in a Grand Lodge to elect a Past Grand Chancellor from among Past Chancellors only; although there is no express, there is an implied prohibition of such action.

1876, Journal, 1283, 1286.

297. Same.

The same rule existed under the old law.

1872, Journal, 469, 575, 613.

298. When Member entitled to Rank of.

Resolved, That hereafter, any Grand Chancellor who has served a full term in that office, and against whom no charges are pending, shall be entitled to the Rank and title of Past Grand Chancellor, as soon as his successor is installed.

1875, Journal, 1034, 1096, 1113, 1121.
1873, Journal, 710, 735.

299. Same.

Resolved, That a Grand Chancellor, on being reelected, shall be entitled to the Rank and title of Past Grand Chancellor immediately after his second installation.

1875, Journal, 1034, 1096, 1113, 1121.

300. When prima facie entitled to Supreme Lodge Rank, etc.

A Grand Chancellor, having served the full term expressed in the law at the time of his election, and holding a certificate to that effect, would prima facie be entitled to admission to the Supreme Lodge; but this does not prevent the Supreme Lodge from refusing entrance to an improper person, or from excluding from admision such an one for matters arising after the issuing of his certificate.

1874, Journal, 945.
1875, Journal, 1127–1129.

301. Rank of, how acquired.

It is inexpedient to provide for any other method, for attaining the Rank of Past Grand Chancellor, than the customary one of service in the chair of Grand Chancellor.

1875, Journal, 1134, 1152.

302. Same.

A Grand Chancellor elected to fill a vacancy, who serves out the balance of the unexpired term, is entitled to the honors of the office.

1874, Journal, 899, 932, 933.

303. Rank of, not to be avoided.

A Grand Lodge, having elected a Past Grand Chancellor, under the law which authorized such an election, and having issued proper credentials thereof, such credentials having been passed upon and approved by the Supreme Lodge, the Grand Lodge cannot thereafter declare such election null and void, and proceed thereupon to elect another to receive said Rank.

1874, Journal, 871, 906, 932.

304. When admitted to Supreme Lodge.

Resolved, That at any subsequent session of the Supreme Lodge, new members shall only be admitted at the opening of the morning sessions on the first two days, and the morning session of the last day.

1875, Journal, 1166.

305. Rank Credentials of.

Ruled by the Supreme Chancellor, that the Past Official Rank of Past Chancellor or Past Grand Chancellor, must be evidenced by a certificate, signed by the proper Grand Officers, duly attested with the Grand Lodge Seal, prior to said Official Rank being recognized, when affiliating by Card in any other Lodge than the one in which being a member where said Rank was attained. (a)

1873, Journal, (Appendix), 36.

(a) See as bearing upon this subject ante, 292, and post, 461, 463, and Article XXIV, Supreme Lodge Constitution.

306. Vacancy in complement of.

A vacancy in the number of Past Grand Chancellors in a Jurisdiction, caused by the suspension of one of said number for a term of years, cannot be filled by the election of another from the Past Chancellors of such Jurisdiction.

1873, Journal, 672, 673.

307. Installation of.

There is no ceremony provided for, or necessary, in passing from the office of Grand Chancellor to the Office and Rank of Past Grand Chancellor.

1873, Journal, 710. 735.

308. When not entitled to be admitted to Supreme Lodge.

A Past Grand Chancellor, in order to be entitled to admission to the Supreme Lodge, must be a member in good standing of a Subordinate Lodge of the Order.

1872, Journal, 444.

309. Admitted in Supreme Lodge without Credentials. Special Case.

On motion of the Representative from a Grand Jurisdiction, a Past Grand Chancellor of the same Jurisdiction admitted and instructed in the Supreme Lodge Rank, although his credentials had never reached the S.K. of R. and S's hands.

1872, Journal, 447.

310. Grand Vice Chancellor not entitled to Honors.

While the laws of the Order confer upon the Grand Vice Chancellor the duties and powers of Grand Chancellor, during the absence, or in case of resignation, removal or death of the Grand Chancellor, for the time being, they do not confer upon him the honors of that office.

1871, Journal, 245, 340.

311. Ruling as to V.G.P., under old Law.

Held, Under the law prior to the adoption of the new Constitution, that upon the reelection of a Grand Chancellor, the then (V.G.P.) Past Grand Chancellor would be entitled to hold over and retain that position another term.

1871, Journal, 380, 392.

312. Credentials, when to be sent to Supreme Lodge.

The Grand Keepers of Records and Seal are required to transmit the credentials of Supreme Representatives and Past Grand Chancellors, at least twenty days before the session of the Supreme Lodge, to the Supreme Keeper of Records and Seal.

1871, Journal, 410.

313. Honors not forfeited.

Under the "Plan" for the organization of the Supreme Lodge, which declared all the then officers of the State Grand Lodges to be Past Grand Chancellors, ruled by the Supreme Lodge, that one of such officers having been admitted a member of the Supreme Lodge, and having been declared by that Body to be a Past Grand Chancellor, did not forfeit those honors by resigning his said office in the Grand Lodge before the expiration of the term thereof.

1868, Journal, 23, 37, 38.

314. Ruling, concerning.

A Grand Chancellor of a State, being such at the date of the adoption of the "Plan" for the organization of the Supreme Lodge, May 15, 1868, and remaining such until the ratification of that "Plan," by the Grand Lodge of said State, although not so continuing until the organization of the Supreme Lodge under said "Plan," *held*, entitled to the Rank of Past Grand Chancellor.

1868, Journal, 41, 45, 47, 59.

PAST SUPREME CHANCELLOR.

315. How Office filled.

Ruled by the Supreme Lodge, that the retiring Supreme Chancellor fills the chair of Past Supreme Chancellor.

1870, Journal, 194.

PUBLIC PARADES.

316. What may be worn in.

Except at funerals, the prescribed Uniform of the Order, with or without Jewels, must be worn in public parade; the collar cannot be worn upon any such occasion.

1875, Journal, 1032, 1096, 1124.

PYTHIAN PERIOD.

317. Commencement of, etc.

Resolved, That hereafter the term "Pythian Period" shall be used immediately after any date given of day, year, or month of the vulgar era, as follows:

"This the ..... day of .... A. D. 187..., and of *Pythian Period* the ...." in all official documents, dispensations, or charters emanating from or issued by this Supreme Lodge or Grand Lodges under its Jurisdiction; and be it further,

Resolved, That the date of the Pythian Period shall date back, and commence on the 19th February, 1864, and each and every year thereafter, and to come, shall succeed in regular numerical order—commencing on the 19th day of February of each year.

1871, Journal, 364, 385.

RAFFLES.

318. Penalties for promoting, etc.

Resolved, That no Grand Lodge, nor Subordinate Lodge, of this Order, nor any individual member of any Lodge, shall, in the name of the Order, resort to, institute or promote, any scheme of raffle, lotteries, gift enterprises, or schemes of chance of any kind. Any Grand Lodge violating this rule, shall forfeit its Charter to the Supreme Lodge. Any Subordinate Lodge violating this rule, shall forfeit its Charter to its Grand Lodge. Any individual member of any Lodge, who shall violate this rule, shall be suspended from the Order.

1876, Journal, 1231, 1264, 1299.

RANKS.

319. When may be conferred by request.

A Subordinate Lodge may confer the Esquire and Knight Ranks on a Page, who has received that Rank in another Lodge, in the same or another Jurisdiction, upon a written official request of his Lodge, certifying that he has received the Rank of Page, and has paid for the other Ranks and been elected thereto. The Lodge conferring those Ranks should send to the Lodge making the request, an official notice of the Ranks having been conferred with date, and he should be entered on their books as holding rank accordingly.

1875, Journal, 1043, 1097, 1114, 1121.

320. When reballot may be had upon application for.

In Subordinate Lodges under the immediate control of the Supreme Lodge, if a Page is rejected on a ballot for the Rank of Esquire, or an Esquire on a ballot for the Rank of Knight, another ballot may be had in either case in one month thereafter.

1875, Journal, 1043, 1097, 1114, 1121.

321. Penalties for refusing to proceed in.

Charges could not be preferred against an Esquire for refusing to proceed any further in the Knight's Rank, after having proceeded through a portion thereof. He would not, however, be entitled to any benefits, privileges or honors of the Knight's Rank.

1875, Journal, 1133, 1140.

322. Title adopted.

The title of "Ranks" in lieu of "Degrees" adopted by the Supreme Lodge.

1872, Journal, 561, 598.

323. Amplified Knight's Rank, how conferred.

Resolved, That the Third or Knight's Rank shall in no instance be conferred according to the * * Amplified Ritual of said Degree as adopted, unless the various parts have been memorized by all the persons officiating therein, so that the same can be conferred without the use of the book.

1872, Journal, 637.

324. Number recognized by Supreme Lodge.

The Supreme Lodge recognizes no higher Rank or Ranks of the Order than the three now established in the Ritual of the Order.

1868, Journal, 17.

REGALIA.

325. Provisions concerning, should not be inserted in Grand Lodge Constitution.

Although it would not be illegal so to do, the provisions of the Supreme Lodge Laws, relative to Regalia, ought not to be introduced into a Grand Lodge Constitution, as any change made in such Laws by the Supreme Lodge, would cause a conflict between the two Laws.

1876, Journal, 1310.

326. What cannot be worn in Public.

The Collar, established as the Regalia of the Order, cannot be worn in a street parade of any character.

1875, Journal, 1032, 1096, 1124.

327. What may be worn at Funerals.

Lodges may appear in public parade, at funerals, wearing the funeral rosette on left breast, with or without Jewels; also in Uniform, with or without Jewels, or in plain citizens' dress.

1875, Journal, 1032, 1096, 1124.

328. Ruling concerning.

The Collar may be worn by Past Officers and Knights in a Lodge Room without the Jewel, but the Uniform never, unless the Collar be also worn.

1875. Journals, 1042, 1097, 1114, 1121.
1872, Journal, 638.

329. Wearing Cap as Regalia.

Resolved, That the Uniform Cap of the Order, as adopted, shall not be worn in a Lodge Room during its sessions, except by order of the Chancellor Commander.

1873, Journal, 683, 734, 740, 742.

330. When Supreme Lodge adopted.

The Regalia for the use of the officers and members of the Supreme Lodge originally adopted.

1868, Journal, 19, 20, 38, 39, 92, 97, 98.

RELIEF BUREAUS.

331. Organizing and Maintaining.

The organizing and maintaining of Relief Bureaus, for the care of sojourning sick members of the Order, is a matter for local legislation.

1873, Journal, 688–690, 722.
1872, Journal, 535, 536, 578.

RITUALS.

332. When originally acted on by Supreme Lodge.

Amendments to the Subordinate Lodge Rituals made by the Supreme Lodge.

1868, Journal, 18, 19, 20, 38, 48.

333. Where to be kept.

The Rituals, and other private work of the Order, should be, and remain in the charge and keeping of the Chancellor Commander of each Lodge, to be kept by him in some safe receptacle, under lock and key, within the Castle Hall of the Lodge, and not to be removed therefrom.

1875, Journal, 1106, 1149, 1152.

334. No part of, to be copied.

All officers and members of Subordinate Lodges are prohibited, by the Supreme Lodge, from in any manner copying any part or parts of the several charges or other Ritualistic ceremonies of the Order.

1875, Journal, 1106, 1134.

335. Memorizing of.

Ruled by the Supreme Chancellor, that it is within the province of the Subordinate Lodge to declare in what space of time officers shall, by memorizing, be able to deliver the charges orally.

1873, Journal, (Appendix), 37.

336. Same.

It is not competent for a Grand Chancellor to require that the Officers of Lodges, in his Jurisdiction, shall memorize the Ritualistic Charges of their offices, within a specified time after the installation, and that thereupon the Rituals shall be delivered to their District Deputy Grand Chancellors, to be retained by them until the next installation of officers.

1873, Journal, 756.

337. Revised and Amplified.

A Revised and Amplified Ritual of the Order, containing the Ritualistic ceremonies for the use of all Subordinate Lodges, together with a designation of the titles, duties and positions of the various officers, adopted by the Supreme Lodge.

1872, Journal, 560, 562, 601, 603, 604, 609, 656-659.

338. Lodges to select Form to use, in certain cases.

Subordinate Lodges have the unqualified right to select for themselves, whether they will use the Amplified Form of the Knight's Rank, or the common form; and Grand Lodges have no right or power to control them in this regard.

1873, Journal, 718.
1872, Journal, 562, 603, 609.

339. Translation of, into other Languages.

The Ritual authorized to be translated into the French language.

1872, Journal, 598, 620.
1873, Journal, (Appendix), 27.
1871, Journal, 379, 386.

340. Same.

Also into the Scandinavian language.

1872, Journal, 622, 623, 628.
1873, Journal, (Appendix), 28, 29.

341. Same.

Also into the Bohemian language.

1871, Journal, 261, 313, 341, 382.
1870, Journal, 186, 191.

342. Same.

Also into the Spanish, Danish, Swedish and all other languages required, at such time as the necessities of the Order require, and the financial condition of the Supreme Lodge warrants.

1871, Journal, 379, 386.
1872, Journal, 598.

343. Same.

Also into the German language.

1868, Journal, 39, 44. 47, 55.
1869, Journal, 86, 107, 116.

344. Same.

Also re-translated into German as soon as the Treasury of the Supreme Lodge will warrant.

1871, Journal, 402, 418.

345. Installation Rituals.

Authorized to be printed in German.

1871, Journal, 381, 383.

346. Installation Rituals.

The Ritual for the installation of officers of Lodges adopted.

1868, Journal, 18, 19, 20, 38, 48.

347. For Supreme Lodge.

The Ritual for the Supreme Lodge adopted.

1868, Journal, 20, 38.

348. For Grand Lodges.

The Ritual for the use of Grand Lodges was adopted.

1868, Journal, 18, 19, 20, 38, 48.

SEAL OF SUPREME LODGE.

349. Copyrighted.

The Seal of the Supreme Lodge was duly copyrighted, and approved as follows:

1875, Journal, 1029, 1116, 1134.

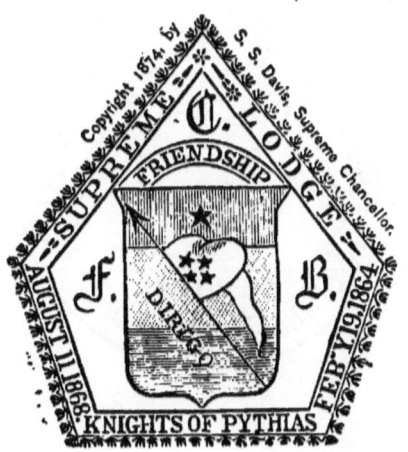

350. Same.

The original copyrighting of the Seal took place June 22, 1870; its form being as above, but the indorsement around it being, "Entered according to Act of Congress in the Clerk's office of the Supreme Court, District of Columbia, by C. M. Barton, June 22, 1870," in place of the present one.

1871, Journal, 263, 313, 341, 382, 383, 428.

351. Adoption of Seal.

The Seal was originally adopted and approved November 10, 1868, being in form as above presented. The "explanation" of the Seal is as follows: The Seal is a polygon—five sided. The five sides represent the five Grand Lodges in existence upon the formation of the Supreme Lodge. On one side the date of the organization of the Supreme Lodge; on the other the date of the foundation of the Order. Over the Shield the word "Friendship," the corner stone of the Order. On the Shield a "flotant," with stars upon it, denoting our ascendency. The perpendicular lines denote the color "Blue"; the dots "Yellow"; the horizontal "Red"; thus showing the colors of the Order. The "Dirigo" means "I guide," or "I direct." Around the Shield is the initials of the mottoes—F. C. and B.

1868, Journal, 25, 45.

352. Of Supreme Chancellor.

An official Seal of the Supreme Chancellor, to be recognized as such, was adopted by the Supreme Lodge as follows:

1873, Journal, 719, 746, (Appendix), 13, 14.

SUPPLIES.

353. Cash to accompany order for.

The Supreme Keeper of Records and Seal is strictly forbidden to deliver any Supplies, to Grand Keepers of Records and Seal, or others, unless the cash accompany the order asking for such Supplies.

1871, Journal, 410.

SUPREME CHANCELLOR.

354. How Hypothetical questions, etc., entertained by.

Resolved, That neither the Supreme Chancellor, nor this Supreme Lodge, will hereafter receive or answer any hypothetical propositions or questions, submitted to them either in recess or during the session of the Supreme Lodge, except the same come from a Grand Lodge, or a Subordinate Lodge under the jurisdiction of this Supreme Lodge, and under the Seal thereof.

1876, Journal, 1311.

355. May issue Dispensation to admit Maimed Person.

Upon application from a Subordinate Lodge, under the immediate jurisdiction of the Supreme Lodge, under its Seal, approved by the Deputy Supreme Chancellor of the the District or Jurisdiction, the Supreme Chancellor may grant a Dispensation for the admission of a maimed person, if in his judgment it appears proper, subject to the same restrictions made to Grand Lodges, as above stated.

1875, Journal, 1040, 1097, 1114, 1121.

356. May rescind S.A.P.W.

The Supreme Chancellor is authorized to rescind the Semi-Annual Password of a Grand Jurisdiction, providing the exigencies of the case demand it.

1875, Journal, 1115, 1116.

357. To retain Grand Lodge Journals.

One copy of the Journals of the various Grand Lodges, upon their being duly bound, to be retained in the office of the Supreme Chancellor.

1875, Journal, 1108, 1124.

358. No power to order general Parade.

The Supreme Chancellor has no power to order a general parade of the whole Order, upon a given time or at a given place.

1874, Journal, 869, 932, 933.

359. Official Seal.

An Official Seal of the Supreme Chancellor, to be recognized as such, was adopted by the Supreme Lodge.   See ante, 352.

1873, Journal, 719, 746, (Appendix), 13, 14.

360. To Commission Deputies.

An Official Commission, to be issued by the Supreme Chancellor, under his Official Seal, to Deputy Supreme Chancellors, was adopted by the Supreme Lodge.

1873, Journal, 680, 719, 746, (Appendix), 12, 13.

361. How to communicate with Subordinate Lodges.

The legal method of communication, from the Supreme authority to the Subordinate Lodges of the several Jurisdiction, where Grand Lodges have been instituted, is through the Grand Lodges.

1872, Journal, 618, 624, 630.

362. Suspending Grand Lodges and Grand Officers.

The suspension of Grand Lodges and a Grand Chancellor, for insubordination, by the Supreme Chancellor during recess, confirmed by the Supreme Lodge.   (a)

1873, Journal, 677, 680, 682; 713-715, (Appendix), 44-73.
1871, Journal, 262-281, 286-288, 290, 291, 340-344, 386-388.

363. Reports to be printed.

Resolved, That the reports of the Supreme Chancellor and Supreme Keeper of Records and Seal, be printed previous to the annual sessions.

1870, Journal, 210.

SUPREME KEEPER OF RECORDS & SEAL.

364. When to have Grand Lodge Journals bound, etc.

As soon as the funds of the Supreme Lodge will permit, the S.K. of R. and S. is authorized to have the Journals of the various Grand Lodges bound; one copy thereof to be retained in his office, and the other in the office of the Supreme Chancellor.

1875, Journal, 1106, 1124.

365. To Supply Memorial Charts.

Resolved, That the Official Memorial Chart and Patent of Membership shall hereafter be furnished by the Supreme Keeper of Records and Seal, to the Grand Keepers of Records

------

(a)   As bearing upon this question, attention is called to Section 6, Article VII, of the present Supreme Lodge Constitution. See post, 541.

and Seal, and through them to the several Subordinate Lodges, in the same manner as all other Supplies.

1875, Journal, 1155.

366. To supply Jewels.

All Jewels of the Order must be procured from the Supreme Keeper of Records and Seal, being regarded as Supplies.

1874, Journal, 972-976.

367. To endeavor to procure reduced fares for Representatives.

The Supreme Keeper of Records and Seal authorized to communicate with the various Railroad Companies, in the various Grand Jurisdictions, in view of securing reduced rates of fare for Supreme Representatives to and from the Supreme Lodge, and to inform the G. K. of R. and S. of the various Jurisdictions of any arrangements thus effected.

1873, Journal, 726.

368. To Submit detailed statements of Supplies, etc.

The Supreme Keeper of Records and Seal is required to submit a detailed statement of Supplies ordered and received by him during the year; also of all Supplies belonging to the Supreme Lodge, that he may have on hand at each annual session.

1874, Journal, 987.
1872, Journal, 824.
1870, Journal, 172, 173.

369. Same, of Expenses, etc.

The Supreme Keeper of Records and Seal is required to furnish annually, to the Supreme Lodge, a detailed and vouched statement of the expenditures, on account of the appropriation for incidental expenses of his office.

1872, Journal, 632, 633.

370. Duty as to furnishing Supplies.

The Supreme Keeper of Records and Seal is strictly forbidden to deliver any Supplies to Grand Keepers of Records and Seal, or others, unless the cash accompany the order asking for such Supplies.

1871, Journal, 410.

371. Reports to be printed.

Resolved, That the reports of the Supreme Chancellor and Supreme Keeper of Records and Seal, be printed previous to the annual sessions.

1870, Journal, 210.

372. Charged with care of Regalia.

The care of the officers' regalia of the Supreme Lodge, especially devolved upon the S. K. of R. and S.

1869, Journal, 100, 121.

373. To notify of approval of Constitutions.

The Supreme Keeper of Records and Seal is required to inform Grand Jurisdictions of the approval of Grand Lodge Constitutions, and instruct the Grand Keepers of Records and Seal to notify Subordinates of such approval. •

1869, Journal, 112.

SUPREME LODGE.

374. What Legislation of, binding.

Resolved, That the legislative acts of the Supreme Lodge, when they accord with the Supreme Lodge Constitution, are binding, and obligatory upon Grand and Subordinate Lodges and members.

1876, Journal, 1232, 1266, 1302.

375. May surrender its Jurisdiction temporarily.

The Supreme Lodge may place any of its Subordinates temporarily under the jurisdiction of a contiguous Grand Lodge, but refuses to allow Grand Lodges to assume extra territorial jurisdiction.

1876. Journal, 1310.
1872, Journal, 620, 621, 627.

376. How Hypothetical Questions, etc., entertained by.

Resolved, That neither the Supreme Chancellor, nor this Supreme Lodge, will hereafter receive or answer any hypothetical propositions or questions, submitted to them either in recess or during the session of the Supreme Lodge, except the same come from a Grand Lodge or a Subordinate Lodge, under the jurisdiction of this Supreme Lodge, and under the Seal thereof.

1876, Journal, 1311.

377. Same.

All such matters, as specified in the last paragraph, are to be presented in proper form to the Committee on Law and Supervision, so far as possible, at least three weeks before the session of the Supreme Lodge; and all matters not presented before the assembling of the Supreme Lodge, to be thereupon presented to the Chairman of the Committee on Law and Supervision, under the penalty, if not so presented, of being subject to pass over to the subsequent session.

1873, Journal, 768.

378. Seal of, copyrighted.

The Seal of the Supreme Lodge was duly copyrighted and approved as follows.

1875, Journal, 1029, 1116, 1134.

379. Same.

The original copyrighting of the Seal took place June 22, 1870; its form being as above; but the indorsement around it being "Entered according to Act of Congress, in the Clerk's office of the Supreme Court, Dist. of Col., by C. M. Barton, June 22, 1870," in place of the present one.

1871, Journal, 261, 313, 341, 382, 383, 428.

380. The head of the Order.

No organization, Lodge, or other collection of men, can be, or have any right to claim to be, any part of the Knights of Pythias, unless they exist under and by virtue of the authority of the Supreme Lodge.

1875, Journal, 1050, 1097, 1141, 1142.

381. When may refuse Admission to P.G.C.

A Grand Chancellor having served the full term expressed in the law at the time of his election, and holding a certificate to that effect, would prima facie be entitled to admission to the Supreme Lodge; but this does not prevent the Supreme Lodge from refusing entrance to an improper person, or from excluding from admission such an one for matters arising after the issuing of his certificate.

1874, Journal, 945.
1875, Journal, 1127-1129.

382. May exclude Members, when.

The Supreme Lodge has the right to eject from its midst one of its members who acts disorderly, contemns its authority, or by his conduct disgraces the Supreme Lodge; and has also the right to prevent the entrance of such an one.

1875, Journal, 1127–1129.

383. Representation in, when forfeited.

Under Articles IX and XVIII, Supreme Lodge Constitution, a Grand Lodge, delinquent as therein specified, does forfeit its right to representation in the Supreme Lodge, but the Supreme Lodge may, by special vote, permit as a privilege (but not as a right) the said Grand Lodge, through its Representatives, to be heard on the floor of the Supreme Lodge.

1875, Journal, 1160, 1164.

384. At what time Members admitted in.

Resolved, That at any subsequent session of the Supreme Lodge, new members shall only be admitted at the opening of the morning sessions on the first two days, and the morning session of the last day.

1875, Journal, 1166.

385. What Laws of, repealed.

The former Constitution under which the Order had worked, and all previous legislation inconsistent with the Constitution adopted on the 25th day of April, 1874, was repealed by the Supreme Lodge on the said date.

1874, Journal, 947.

386. Curative Acts passed by the Supreme Lodge.

Legalizing the institution and work of Metropolitan Lodge of Montreal, P. Q.

1874, Journal, 930, 931.
1875, Journal, 1035–1037, 1116, 1125.

387. Same.

Legalizing the work of the Grand and Subordinate Lodges of Pennsylvania and their officers, during the time of the troubles growing out of the promulgation of the new Amplified Ritual.

1873, Journal, 713, 714, 715, 718, 719, 769.

388. Same.

Legalizing election of Grand Officers of Pennsylvania. The election and installation of the officers of the Grand Lodge of Pennsylvania, confirmed and approved upon their complying with the legislation of the Supreme Lodge.

1871, Journal, 428.

389. Same.

Legalizing the admission of a member under age, but the same never to be considered as a precedent for like action in the future.

1870, Journal, 140, 191, 192.

390. When Past Grand Chancellor entitled to admission.

A Past Grand Chancellor, in order to be entitled to admission to the Supreme Lodge, must be a member in good standing of a Subordinate Lodge of the Order.

1872, Journal, 444.

391. Representatives conceded privileges.

A Grand Lodge being indebted to the Supreme Lodge, but time being given to make payment, the Supreme Representatives from the Jurisdiction conceded like privileges in the Supreme Lodge as others.

1872, Journal, 447.

392. Same.

The Representatives from a Grand Jurisdiction indebted to the Supreme Lodge, conceded all the rights and privileges of the floor of the Supreme Lodge, notwithstanding their indebtedness.

1872, Journal, 538.

393. P.G.C. admitted without Credentials; special case.

On motion of the Representative from a Grand Jurisdiction, a Past Grand Chancellor of the same Jurisdiction admitted and instructed in the Supreme Lodge Rank, although his credentials had never reached the S. K. of R. and S's. hands.

1872, Journal, 447.

394. Representatives admitted on Telegram.

A Supreme Representative admitted to his seat in the Supreme Lodge, upon a telegram showing his appointment to such position.

1875, Journal, 1095 1096.

395. How to communicate with Subordinate Lodges.

The legal method of communication from the Supreme authority to the Subordinate Lodges of the several Jurisdictions, where Grand Lodges have been instituted, is through the Grand Lodge.

1872, Journal, 618, 624, 630.

396. Alternate Representatives.

There is no law in the Order authorizing the election of alternate Representatives to the Supreme Lodge.

1871, Journal, 342, 343.

397. Drawing for Seats.

At the commencement of each session of the Supreme Lodge, a committee is to be appointed, who shall draw for seats to be occupied by the Representatives of the several Jurisdictions.

1871, Journal, 428.

398. Election of Officers.

Ruled by the Supreme Lodge, that although Supreme Lodge Officers were required to be elected by ballot, still it was competent, in cases where there was but one nominee for an office, to authorize by motion, one member to cast the vote of the Supreme Lodge for such nominee.

1870, Journal, 194, 195, 196.

399. Same.

Notwithstanding such motion however, it is still the right of every member of the Supreme Lodge present to vote for such officer if he desires so to do.

1870, Journal, 194, 195, 196.

400. Mileage of Officers.

Ruled by the Supreme Lodge, that newly elected, as well as the retiring officers of the Supreme Lodge, are entitled to mileage, provided, that no one shall receive mileage both as an Officer and a Representative.

1870, Journal, 197, 198, 221.

401. Minutes, when read and acted on.

The proceedings of each session to be read and considered at the commencement of the next morning and afternoon session thereafter, respectively.

1870, Journal, 219.

402. Resolutions, etc., how presented.

Resolved, That at the future sessions of the Supreme Lodge, all resolutions and motions of length be written upon half sheet letter paper, in legible hand writing, folded twice and properly backed, with a title referring to the subject matter contained therein, and the signature of the member offering the same.

1870, Journal, 224.

403. Ritual adopted.

The Ritual for the Supreme Lodge was adopted.

1868, Journal, 20, 38.

404. Resolution as to Mileage.

No Supreme Lodge Officer or Representative shall receive his mileage and expenses, unless he is present at the close of the session, or is excused by the Supreme Chancellor.

1869, Journal, 94.

SUPREME REPRESENTATIVE.

405. Who eligible to election as.

Any Grand Chancellor, who has served a full term in that office, and against whom no charges are pending, shall be entitled to the Rank and title of Past Grand Chancellor as soon as his successor is installed, and is thereupon eligible to election as Supreme Representative, but not before.

1876, Journal, 1194, 1266, 1267.
1875, Journal, 1113, 1121.
1874, Journal, 900, 908.

406. Same.

Upon reelection, a Grand Chancellor after his second installation, is entitled to the Rank of Past Grand Chancellor. No one is eligible to election as Supreme Representative until he is entitled to the Rank of P. G. C.

1876, Journal, 1194, 1266, 1267.
1875, Journal, 1034, 1113, 1121.

407. Terms of, when commencing, and when ending.

The terms of Supreme Representatives fixed for the Calendar year; that from January 1st to December 31st.

1876, Journal, 1229, 1266, 1296.

408. Should not be deprived of his Office without Trial.

The seat of a Supreme Representative, as a general proposition, should not be declared vacant, except as the result of a fair and impartial trial.

1875, Journal, 1003, 1122.

409. When admitted to Supreme Lodge.

Resolved, That at any subsequent session of the Supreme Lodge, new members shall only be admitted at the opening of the morning sessions on the first two days, and the morning session of the last day.

1875, Journal, 1166.

410. Appointment of.

The Supreme Representatives, appointed by the Grand Chancellor of a Grand Lodge under a clause in the Constitution thereof, providing that the Grand Chancellor might "appoint Grand Officers (a) pro tem., in case of the temporary absence or disqualification of any Grand Officer," were admitted by the Supreme Lodge to their seats, it appearing that the Grand Lodge had adjourned without electing Representatives.

1872, Journal, 442–444.

(a) At the time of this action, by the Constitutions of Grand Lodges, Supreme Representatives were officers of the Grand Lodge; whether the ruling would be upheld under the present Constitution, is a question.

411. Same.

The Constitution of the Supreme Lodge provides for the election of Representatives, and they cannot otherwise be chosen, even to fill a vacancy, unless in pursuance of the Laws of a Grand Lodge, adopted for that purpose.

1872, Journal, 442, 443.

412. Conceded privileges.

A Grand Lodge being indebted to the Supreme Lodge, but time being given to make payment, the Supreme Representatives from the Jurisdiction conceded like privileges in the Supreme Lodge as others.

1872, Journal, 447.

413. Same.

The Representatives from a Grand Jurisdiction, indebted to the Supreme Lodge, conceded all the rights and privileges of the floor of the Supreme Lodge, notwithstanding their indebtedness.

1872, Journal, 538.

414. Admitted on Telegram, special case.

A Supreme Representative admitted to his seat in the Supreme Lodge, upon a telegram showing his appointment to such position.

1875, Journal, 1095, 1096.

415. From newly constructed Grand Lodge.

A Grand Lodge having been suspended by the Supreme Chancellor for insubordination, and another Grand Lodge having been instituted the same as in a new Jurisdiction, the Representatives from the newly constructed Grand Lodge admitted to the Supreme Lodge.

1871, Journal, 262–275, 290, 291, 342, 386-388.

416. Alternates.

There is no law in the Order authorizing the election of alternate Representatives to the Supreme Lodge.

1871, Journal, 342, 343.

417. Credentials, when to be sent to Supreme Lodge.

The Grand Keepers of Records and Seal are required to transmit the credentials of Supreme Representatives and Past Grand Chancellors, at least twenty days before the session of the Supreme Lodge, to the Supreme Keeper of Records and Seal.

1871, Journal, 410.

418. Resolution as to Mileage.

No Supreme Lodge Officer or Representative shall receive his mileage and expenses, unless he is present at the close of the session, or is excused by the Supreme Chancellor.

1869, Journal, 94.

TAXATION.

419. For what purposes allowable.

If in accordance with its Constitution, a Grand Lodge may provide that a certain portion of the semi-annual per capita tax levied upon the Subordinate Lodges, may be set aside as a Sinking Fund, for the purpose of building a "Castle" for the use of the Order.

1875, Journal, 1102, 1148, 1149.

TRAVELING SHIELDS.

420. Dues to be paid upon receipt of.

A member receiving a Traveling Shield is only required to pay dues for the length of time covered by the Shield.

1875, Journal, 1015-1022, 1096, 1099, 1144-1146.

421. How regarded.

The Traveling Shield is only regarded as evidence of the good standing of the holder in his Lodge, and as a letter of credit or Relief Shield.

1875, Journal, 1015-1022, 1096, 1099, 1106, 1144-1146.

422. To whom cannot issue

A member holding a Withdrawal Card, is not entitled to a Traveling Shield.

1875, Journal, 1042, 1097, 1114, 1116, 1121.

423. Adopted and particulars concerning.

A Traveling Shield was originally adopted, and full particulars as to its form and manner of issue and use provided, as will appear by the following references.

1874, Journal, 969-973.
1873, Journal, 696, 771-773.

TRIALS.

424. Always to be given.

A party's rights should not, as a general proposition, be forfeited in any case, only as the result of a fair and impartial trial.

1875, Journal, 1003, 1102, 1122, 1127-1129.

425. How to be conducted in Grand Lodge.

As a general proposition, there are no written rules or declaratory law for conducting proceedings upon charges against a Grand Lodge Officer. The right to try, to suspend, or even to remove from office, do of necessity exist, and there is no impropriety, in the absence of specific written rules, in using as a guide, for the action of a Grand Lodge, the laws prescribed for the government of Subordinate Lodges in analagous cases.

1874, Journal, 861-868, 945.
1875, Journal, 1127-1129.

426. May be prosecuted in Grand Lodge.

The Grand Lodge holds jurisdiction over its own members, and when charges are preferred against them as such, all Laws, operative there or in the Subordinate Lodge, are applicable, until the matter is fully determined. So ruled by the Supreme Chancellor.

1873, Journal, (Appendix), 37.

UNIFORM.

427. When may be worn with Collar.

A Knight may wear the Uniform in connection with the Collar, during the regular Lodge Conventions.

1872, Journal, 638.

428. Ruling concerning.

The Uniform, unaccompanied with the Collar, can never be worn, even by Knights, as Regalia in a Lodge Room, without the Jewel. Officers must always wear the Jewel.

1875, Journal, 1042, 1097, 1114, 1121.
1874, Journal, 901, 908.
1873, Journal, (Appendix), 36.
1872, Journal, 614, 615, 627, 638, Con. Sup. Lodge, Art. XXX.

429. To be used for the Order.

The members of the Order are only permitted to use the Uniform when performing duties requiring the same, and upon occasions connected with the Order.

1875, Journal, 1154, 1156.

430. Cap not to be worn in Lodge.

Resolved, That the Uniform Cap of the Order as adopted, shall not be worn in a Lodge room during its sessions, except by order of the Chancellor Commander.

1873, Journal, 683, 734, 740, 742.

431. To be worn on Public Parades.

Except at funerals, the prescribed Uniform of the Order, with or without Jewels, must be worn in public parade; the collar cannot be worn upon any such occasion.

1875, Journal, 1032, 1096, 1124.

432. Adoption of Uniform.

The Uniform of the Order for outside uses, pursuant to details duly presented and set forth, was originally recommended for use where practicable or desirable, subject to the final adoption of the different Grand Lodges of the various Jurisdictions.

> 1871, Journal, 362, 396, 409.
> 1872, Journal, 484-500.

433. Same.

Subsequently the Uniform recommended as above, with the exception of the Helmet, Oriflamme, Gorget and Cloak, was declared the Permanent Uniform or Outside Regalia for the use of the Order, not subject to change, mutilation or reduction for the space of ten years from the date of the session of the Supreme Lodge of 1872.

> 1872, Journal, 577, 578, 589, 590, 600, 630.

434. Helmet.

The details of the Helmet will be found by the following references :

> 1875, Journal, 1098, 1135, 1159.
> 1874, Journal, 912, 983, 984.
> 1873, Journal, 692, 694-696, 706-709, 770.

435. Specifications as to Uniform, etc.

The following are the detailed specifications of the Uniform as at present existing :

436. Full Gala and Inspection Dress.

Coat, Pants, Sword, Belt, Baldric, Cloak (a), Gorget (a), Gauntlet Cuffs, Gloves, Helmet (a), and Oriflamme (a), (with Fatigue Cap, covered, hung to Belt.)

437. Ordinary Parade Dress.

Coat, Pants, Sword, Belt, Baldric, Gauntlet Cuffs, Gloves, Helmet (a), and Oriflamme (a), (with Fatigue Cap, covered, suspended from Sword Belt.)

438. Fatigue Dress.

Coat, Pants, Sword, Belt, Fatigue Cap, (uncovered) and White Gloves.

439. Coat.

Black cloth, cut military style, single breasted, standing collar, (with a half roll to the sixth button from the bottom)

(a) Under the legislation as referred to, by which the Uniform was adopted, the use of these articles, it would seem, was left entirely discretionary with Grand Lodges. If used, however, they must be the ones adopted by the Supreme Lodge.

nine buttons in front, two behind, length to knee, side edges plain, hook-and-eye at neck gorge, seam plain, two buttons at cuff, button flat black silk lasting.

ORDINARY PARADE DRESS.

440. Pantaloons.

Black cloth, or doeskin cassimere, and of uniform style.

FULL PARADE AND INSPECTION DRESS.

NOTE.—For the purpose of giving a full showing of detail of points in the uniform, the swords in the cuts have been shown as they appear in them, but which is *incorrect*. The swords are hanging from and by chains from the belt, running to rings placed on either side of the scabbard, about *two and one half inches* below the hilt of sword, when in its sheath, and which, when in proper place, hang *perpendicular*. See cut of sword and belt.

441. Cloak.

A half-cloak—*a cavalier*—or cape of appropriate material, make and color, emblazoned thereon, embroidered on proper colored cloth or velvet, the crest of the Order, to be worn over the left shoulder and back fastened by a cord and tassel of appropriate color. The "Gorget" worn with the same made of *three* triangular points; one of which will be *scarlet*, one *sky blue*, and one *orange*. Pendant to the point of each proper color will be the appropriate letter, in *solid* white metal. The *Gorget* to be separate, and fastened on by buttoning under collar of cape or by cord and tassel.

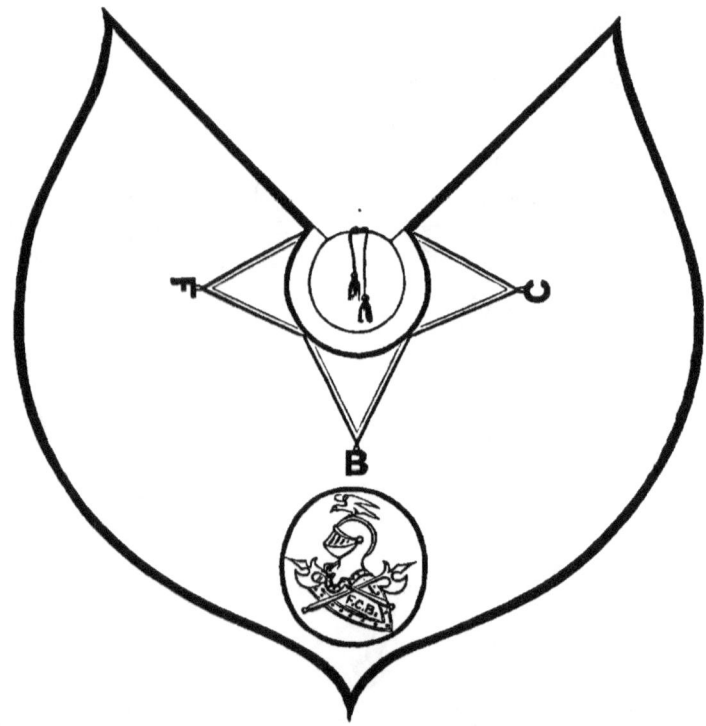

For Members and Subordinate Officers, inclusive of Worthy Chancellor; Cloak *dark blue*, crest *scarlet*.

For Past Chancellors and Grand Officers, (of less rank than Grand Chancellor); Cloak *orange*, crest *blue*.

For Grand and Past Grand Chancellors; Cloak *scarlet*, crest *blue*.

For Supreme and Past Supreme Chancellors; Cloak *purple*, crest *gold*.

442 Helmet.

Black body, in shape like sample; round top, rim in front and flowing back; front vizor 2 inches and rear vizor $2\frac{1}{2}$ inches length; black cone, running from tip of back to center front; cone $2\frac{1}{2}$ inches high in front, running back to point at tip of flowing back; raised wire for plume support, from back tip to front of cone, one-half inch above cone. Gold (or silver) cord, double and looped from center sides to front, fastened at sides with Helmet-shaped button.

ESCUTCHEON ON FRONT AS FOLLOWS:—For Knights—Shield-shaped escutcheon, $1\frac{1}{2}$ inches.

For Past Chancellors (less rank than G. C.)—Triangle-shaped escutcheon, 2 inches from tip to tip.

For Grand Chancellor and Past Grand Chancellor—Oval-shaped escutcheon, 2 inches in shortest diameter.

For Supreme Officers and Past Supreme Officers—Circular-shaped escutcheon, 2 inches in diameter.

PLUME.—In shape an Oriflamme, running from back of cone to front, and drooping over front, to be worn as follows:

For Knights—Red.

For Past Chancellors—Blue.

For Grand Lodge Officers—Yellow.

For Past Grand Chancellors—Red, tipped (on sides and front) with white.

For Supreme Officers and Past Supreme Officers—Purple, tipped with white (on sides and front.)

DISTINCTIONS.—Knights and Past Chancellors (of less rank than Grand Chancellor) will wear white metal or silver; Grand Chancellors and Past Grand Chancellors will wear yellow metal or gold.

443. Cap.

Present navy style, black cloth, three to three and one-half inches height of crown, narrow, black leather straps fastened at sides with shield-shaped buttons. The crest or escutcheon of the Order on the front, and gold or silver lace running around the band of the Cap, according to rank of wearer.

ESCUTCHEON AND LACE.

For Knights, Esquires and Pages, silver-plated METAL, shield-shaped escutcheon, and 3 LIGNE silver lace.

For Subordinate Officers, inclusive of Worthy Chancellors, shield-shaped EMBROIDERED escutcheon, on BLUE velvet and 6 LIGNE silver lace.

For Past Chancellors, shield-shaped, EMBROIDERED escutcheon, on GREEN velvet and 6 LIGNE silver lace.

For Grand Officers, inclusive of G. C., shield-shaped, EMBROIDERED escutcheon, on ORANGE velvet and 9 LIGNE silver lace.

For Past Grand Chancellors, oval-shaped, EMBROIDERED escutcheon, on RED velvet and 12 LIGNE gold lace.

For Supreme and Past Supreme Chancellors, circular-shaped, EMBROIDERED escutcheon, with vine around, and S. C., or P. S. C., on PURPLE and 15 LIGNE gold lace.

444. Baldric.

To be worn by all members of less rank than Grand Chancellors. Five inches wide, in the whole, of blue bordered with yellow, one inch on either side, a strip of army lace one-fourth of an inch wide at the inner edge of the yellow. On the front centre of the Baldric, a metal triangle with raised—or struck up—escutcheon of the Order. On centre field of the triangle, and on each uncovered point thereof, one of the three letters " F. C. B.," so that the whole three may appear. The Baldric to be worn from the right shoulder to the left hip, with ends extending six inches below the point of intersection, under and at the lower edge of the sword belt, and be fastened with shield-shaped white metal screw button, the top of which will overlap the sword belt, and hold the Baldric firmly in its place on the right shoulder.

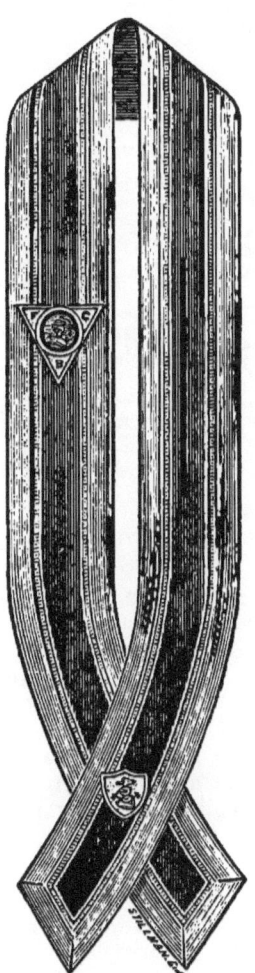

BALDRIC.

445. Belt.

Red enameled or patent leather two inches wide, fastened around the body with white metal clasp of emblematic design, two short white metal chains suspended from red leather sliding straps on belt, and white metal slide, with hook, for Fatigue Cap.

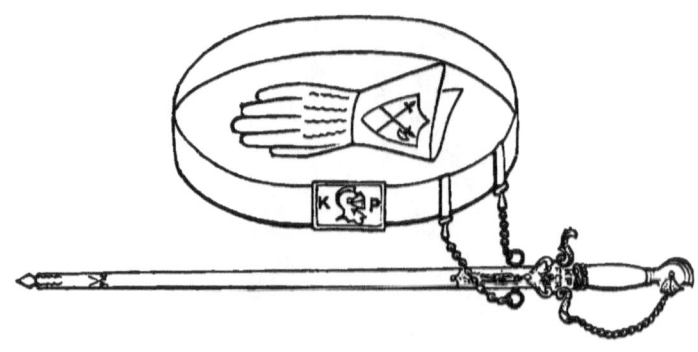

SWORD.

For all members and officers (of less rank than Grand Chancellor) thirty-four to forty inches long, white metal scabbard, cross handle black hilt; Helmet head with appropriate devices, suspended by chains from two side rings.

For all Officers and Past Officers, from rank of Grand Chancellor up, same as above, except gilt in place of white metal, and white instead of black grip.

446. Gauntlets.

Black leather, military style, cuff to extend four and one-half inches up from its intersection with the hand, and to have a shield-shaped metal escutcheon of the Order (two inches in length) on back of cuff, or, black kid gloves with patent leather cuffs (of proper length and color), separate or together, as most convenient to wearer (and in fatigue dress white gloves WITHOUT the cuffs). Knights, Chancellors and Grand Officers (of less rank that Grand Chancellor) SILVER-plated escutcheons. Grand, Past Grand Chancellors, and Supreme and Past Supreme Chancellors, GOLD-plated escutcheons.

447. Emblems of Official Rank.

SHOULDER STRAPS FOR OFFICERS.

SUPREME AND PAST SUPREME CHANCELLORS.

Royal purple silk velvet, four inches long by two inches wide, outside measurement, bordered with *three* rows of corded embroidery in GOLD, each one-eighth of an inch wide, the escutcheon or *crest* of the Order at each end, and globe or world in centre. The Past Supreme Chancellors same as S. C., and to have in addition three small stars in silver, one at the centre of top, and one each at the right and left corners at the foot of the strap.

All other Supreme Officers same size, color and embroidery as Supreme Chancellor's, with the exception of the escutcheon or crest at the ends, in place of which the initials (in old English characters) of their office, as equally divided as possible, at each end of the strap, *all in gold.*

PAST GRAND CHANCELLORS.

Bright red silk velvet, four inches long by two inches wide, with *two* rows of corded embroidery each one-eighth of an inch wide, and escutcheon or crest of the Order embroidered in the middle *in gold*, and the letters "P. G. C.," (in old English characters,) embroidered *in silver* on the lower end of the strap.

GRAND CHANCELLORS.

Bright orange silk velvet, same size and embroidery as "P. G. C's," except in centre is embroidered, in silver, a gauntlet closed and grasping the truncheon of office, and at lower end of strap, *in silver*, (in old English characters) the letters "G. C."

ALL OTHER GRAND OFFICERS.

Same size, design, color, shape, and embroidery as G. C., except in centre of strap a shield (instead of gauntlet, etc.), and at the lower end (in old English characters) the initials of their office, but *all in silver.*

PAST CHANCELLORS.

Bright emerald green silk velvet three and one-half inches long by one and one-half inches wide, bordered with one row of embroidery, one quarter inch wide, crossed battle axes in centre, and letters "P. C.," (in old English characters) at lower end, *all in silver.*

WORTHY CHANCELLOR.

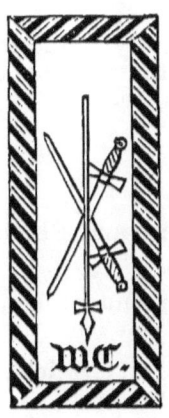

Bright blue silk velvet, same size and design as Past Chancellor in other respects, except in centre is embroidered *in silver*, crossed swords and a hand-lance *in gold*, running lengthwise of the strap through the swords, head towards the foot, and the letters "W. C." (in old English characters) at the foot of the strap, *in silver*.

VICE CHANCELLOR.

The same as *W. C.* except, instead of crossed swords in centre, is simply a tilting lance, running LENGTHWISE, head towards the foot of strap, and letters "W." and "V." in centre, on either side of lance, and "C." at foot of the same, covered by head of the lance, ALL IN SILVER.

OTHER SUBORDINATE LODGE OFFICERS.

Same as W. C. and V. C. in color and embroidery, on edges, no design, but with simply the letters (in old English) or initials indicative of the various offices, in TRIANGULAR arrangement in the centre.

448. Arms.

For PAGES—Battle-Axe and Shield, of appropriate make and material.

For ESQUIRES—Lance and Shield, of appropriate make and material.

For KNIGHTS—Sword and Shield, as prescribed, and of appropriate make and material.

For OFFICERS and PAST OFFICERS—Swords, as heretofore prescribed.

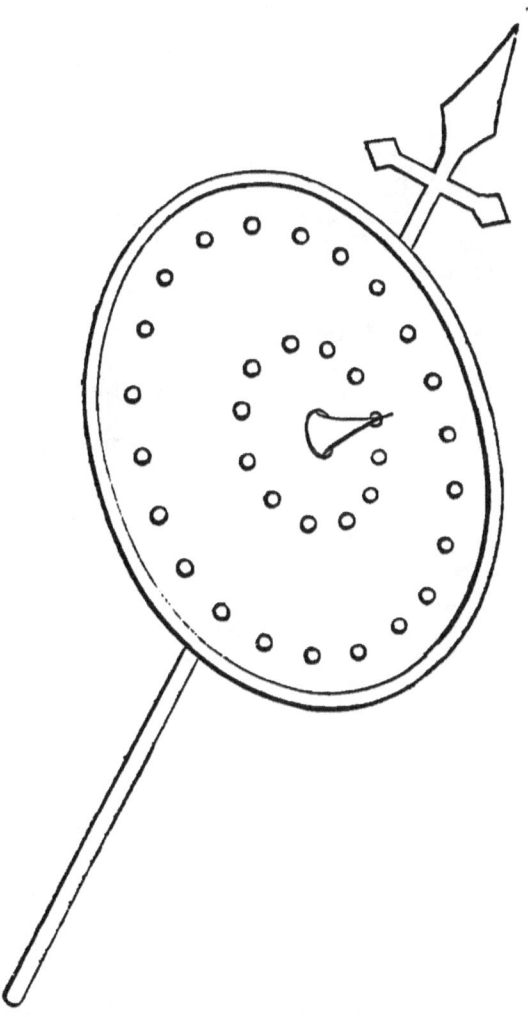

DISTINCTIONS.

Pages, Esquires, Knights, Chancellors, Past Chancellors and Grand Officers (of less rank than Grand Chancellor). will wear WHITE METAL or SILVER wherever metal, embroidery, or lace appears, unless otherwise specifically stated. Grand and Past Grand Chancellors, Supreme and Past Supreme Officers, YELLOW METAL or GOLD, wherever metal, embroidery or lace appears, unless otherwise specifically stated.

449. Not compulsory.

The subject of uniforming is left entirely voluntary with the Order everywhere.

1872, Journal, 577, 578, 600.

VICE CHANCELLOR.

450. To inspect ballot.

A ballot for a candidate for membership should be inspected by the Vice Chancellor, and the result announced by the Chancellor Commander.

1876, Journal, 1227, 1266, 1296.

451. Who eligible to Office of.

Any Knight in good standing, having served one term in any elective or appointive office, is eligible to the office of Vice Chancellor.

1875, Journal, 1033, 1096, 1124.

VISITATIONS.

452. Cannot be interfered with.

Objections cannot be made to a member in good standing, and otherwise correct, while visiting another Lodge. If any one is satisfied the visitor is unworthy to sit in a Lodge Room, he must proceed against him under the penal laws of the Order, or keep silent.

1875, Journal, 1042, 1097, 1114, 1116,1121.

453. By Lodge as a Body.

It is competent for the Chancellor Commander of a Lodge, to appoint the Master-at-Arms to receive the Password in the ante-room, from members of a visiting Lodge, after each of the visiting Knights have worked their way through the outer door, and the Lodge can then be admitted as a body.

1874, Journal, 913, 935.

454. Not to be made on Withdrawal Card.

Ruled by the Supreme Chancellor, that Withdrawal Cards could not, and must not, be used for, or recognized in any sense as visiting credentials.

1873, Journal, (Appendix), 36.

455. Made by Person holding Withdrawal Card.

Ruled by the Supreme Chancellor, that a member holding a Withdrawal Card was entitled to the semi-annual Password for the term in which issued, and inferentially to visit Lodges on such Password during such term.

1873, Journal, (Appendix), 36.
1872, Journal, 467, 575, 612, 613.

WITHDRAWAL CARD.

456. Member holding, when may apply for Membership.

A member holding a Withdrawal Card, in force, applying to a Lodge for membership, by deposit of same, and being rejected, may apply again to any other Lodge, or, in the absence of any local law, to the same Lodge, at any time.

1876, Journal, 1228, 1266, 1296.

457. A Lodge cannot reconsider a Vote granting.

A Lodge cannot, at the request of the holder of a Withdrawal Card or otherwise, reconsider or rescind the vote granting such card.

1876, Journal, 1228, 1266, 1296, 1297.

458. For what Time good.

Resolved, That Withdrawal Cards be considered good until revoked or deposited, and that all legislation inconsistent herewith be repealed.

1876, Journal, 1309, 1310.

459. Not limited to one year.

There is no reason for limiting to one year, the time upon which a Knight, who has severed his connection with a Lodge, may deposit his Card and renew his membership in the Order.

1876, Journal, 1227, 1228, 1266, 1309, 1310.

460. Rank of Member to be stated. (a)

Resolved, That the Rank of a Brother, to whom a Withdrawal Card is issued, shall be stated on the Card, and that the form of the Card shall be altered to conform to this legislation.

1876, Journal, 1231, 1266, 1309, 1310.

461. Insufficiency of, as Rank Credential. (b)

Ruled by the Supreme Chancellor, that Withdrawal Cards evidence no Rank in the Order of higher grade than that of Knight, and any prefix or affix thereto, setting forth that the bearer is a Past Chancellor or Past Grand Chancellor, is void and of no value as a credential of those two higher grades of Rank.

1873, Journal, (Appendix), 10, 35.

462. Grand Lodge cannot compel Renewal of.

A Grand Lodge cannot compel a Subordinate Lodge to renew a Withdrawal Card, when its By-Laws provide that such renewal can only be obtained upon a ballot, two balls rejecting the application.

1876, Journal, 1284, 1300.

(a) See as bearing on this subject ante 292, 305, post 461, 463 and Article XXIV, Supreme Lodge Constitution, post 593.

(b) See as bearing on this subject ante 292, 305 and post 463, also Article XXIV, Supreme Lodge Constitution, post 593.

463. As to placing Past Rank upon. (a)

Under the terms of a Constitution providing "That a Past Chancellor, previous to being admitted as a member of the Grand Lodge, must present a certificate from his Lodge, certifying that he had passed the Chair of his Lodge;" ruled, that a Grand Lodge erred in requiring a Lodge to place "P.C." upon a Withdrawal Card, issued to a member of such Lodge.

1876, Journal, 1306.

464. Page, when entitled to.

A Page having become such in a Lodge that thereafter becomes extinct, wishing to connect himself with the Order in another Jurisdiction, would be entitled to a Card issued from the Grand Lodge, under the Jurisdiction of which he was a member, which he would be entitled to deposit in another Jurisdiction as in other cases.

1876, Journal, 1311, 1314.

465. Holder of, not entitled to Traveling Shield.

A member holding a Withdrawal Card is not entitled to a Traveling Shield.

1875, Journal, 1042, 1097, 1114, 1116, 1121.

466. Not to be used for Visiting.

Ruled by the Supreme Chancellor, that Withdrawal Cards could not, and must not, be used for, or recognized in any sense as visiting credentials.

1873, Journal, (Appendix), 36.

467. As to Visitations by Member holding.

Ruled by the Supreme Chancellor, that a member holding a Withdrawal Card was entitled to the Semi-annual Password for the term in which issued, and inferentially to visit Lodges on such Password during such term.

1873, Journal, (Appendix), 36.
1872, Journal, 467, 575, 612, 613.

468. To whom should not issue.

Ruled by the Supreme Chancellor, that a Past Chancellor upon trial in the Grand Lodge, should not be granted a Withdrawal Card by his Subordinate Lodge.

1873, Journal, (Appendix), 37.

469. When to be Annulled, etc.

Ruled by the Supreme Chancellor, that a Card improvidently issued to a Past Chancellor, while under charges in his Grand Lodge, can be recalled or annulled by action of the Lodge or order of the Grand Chancellor.

1873, Journal, (Appendix), 37.

(a) Upon this subject see Supreme Lodge Constitution, of Article XXIV, also legislation of Supreme Lodge, ante 292, 305, 461.

WORK, WRITTEN AND UNWRITTEN.

470. What portions of, cannot be changed, except by four-fifths Vote, etc.

The Written and Unwritten Work that cannot be changed except by a four-fifth vote, and after having laid over from one regular session of the Supreme Lodge to another, consists:

1. Of the Work and its Explanations, as contained and illustrated in the Book of Diagrams, in the hands of the Supreme Chancellor.

2. Of the Lectures, Charges, Obligations, and all Written Work contained in the Ritual, and included in the forms and ceremonies for opening and closing the Lodge, passing from Rank to Rank, and conferring the different grades of Rank.

3. The forms and ceremonies as prescribed for Installation and Funeral.

4. The forms and ceremonies, as prescribed for opening and closing a Grand Lodge, and installing the officers thereof, as contained in the Grand Lodge Ritual, and also for conferring P.C.'s Rank, as contained in the same.

5. The forms and ceremonies, as laid down in Supreme Lodge Rituals.

1876, Journal, 1282, 1293.

471. When may be given outside of Lodge Room.

A Grand Chancellor, or his Deputy, can give instruction in the secret work outside of a Lodge Room, and can also give the Semi-annual Password to a Chancellor Commander.

1873, Journal, 703, 723.

472. Diagrams of Secret Work.

Pursuant to action of the Supreme Lodge, the whole of the Secret Work of the Order has been properly written out and correct diagrams of the same prepared.

1872, Journal, 465, 531, 575, 594.
1873, Journal, 719, 720, 752 (Appendix), 29, 30.
1875, Journal, 1050, 1095, 1097, 1108, 1147, 1157.

INCORPORATION.

473. Certificate of Association of the Supreme Lodge, Knights of Pythias.

WHEREAS, It is deemed advisable to have the Supreme Lodge of Knights of Pythias an incorporated body, under the laws of the Congress of the United States, for the more perfect working of the benificent intentions of the said Order.

474.

AND WHEREAS, With a view to promote this object, and as Grand and Subordinate Lodges of the said Order have been formed or organized in various States and Territories, and will be hereafter formed in various other States and Territories of the United States, as well as foreign countries.

475.

1. Now, therefore, be it known, That in accordance with the Act of Congress, entitled "An Act to provide for the creation of Corporations in the District of Columbia, by general law," approved May 5, 1870, the undersigned having associated themselves for the purpose, and with the design, of establishing and creating the Corporation to be known and named the Supreme Lodge Knights of Pythias, do hereby make and authorize to be filed in the office of the Register of Deeds, in the District of Columbia, this certificate and these Articles of Association for the government of themselves, their associates, assigns and successors.

476.

2. And be it further known, That the beneficial association, of which this is the certificate, shall be known as the Supreme Lodge of the Knights of Pythias, the Seal of which has been copyrighted by the Supreme Recording and Corresponding Scribe in the Clerk's Office of the Supreme Court of the District of Columbia, [and has also been recorded in the Office of the Librarian of Congress, in the Capitol of the United States, at Washington, D. C.].

477.

3. [The Supreme Lodge shall consist of all Past Supreme Chancellors, the Supreme Officers, and two Representatives from each Grand Lodge, under the jurisdiction of said Supreme Lodge until there are 20,000 members under the jurisdiction of a Grand Lodge, and one Supreme Representative for each additional 10,000 members. Provided, that no Grand Lodge shall be entitled to more than four (4) Supreme Representatives.]

478.

4. [The Board of Trustees shall consist of Supreme Chancellor, S. S. Davis, of New Hampshire; S. K. of R. and S.,

Joseph Dowdall, of Ohio; S. M. of E., John B. Stumph, of Indiana, and Supreme Vice Chancellor, D. B. Woodruff, of Georgia; who shall serve until the election of their successors, it being understood that the four principal officers of the Supreme Lodge shall compose the Board of Trustees.]

479.

[5.] And be it further known, That the Officers of the said Supreme Lodge, Knights of Pythias of the World, shall consist of [Past Supreme Chancellor], Supreme Chancellor, Supreme Vice Chancellor, [Supreme Keeper of Records and Seal, Supreme Master of Exchequer, Supreme Master at Arms, Supreme Inner Guard, Supreme Outer Guard,] all of whom shall be elected by ballot every alternate year [****] and the said Supreme Keeper of Records and Seal and Supreme Master of Exchequer shall give such security, for the faithful performance of their duty, as may be ordered by said Supreme Lodge.

480.

[6.] That the said Supreme Lodge shall hold an annual session, at such time and place as a majority of its members present may determine, for the transaction of all business for the benefit and welfare of the Order, and that the Supreme Chancellor may, and on the call of the Supreme Representatives of ten Grand Jurisdictions in writing, shall convene an extra session of said Supreme Lodge at Washington City, D. C.

481.

[7.] And be it further known, That a Representative from a majority of the Grand Lodges, working under the jurisdiction of this Supreme Lodge, shall constitute a quorum for the transaction of business.

482.

[8.] And be it further known, That the said Supreme Lodge have the power to alter and amend its Constitution and By-Laws at will, and that it shall have power to prescribe modes of initiation, etc., for the working of said Order; and no Grand or Subordinate Lodges, purporting to be Knights of Pythias, shall have legal standing unless chartered by, or through, the regularly elected officers of this Supreme Lodge in regular or called sessions, or by the Supreme Chancellor during the recess of the Supreme Lodge.

483.

[And it is hereby declared, that, all and singular, the parts of the incorporation of August 5, 1870, not altered by this supplementary paper, are hereby ratified and reaffirmed, and that said Supreme Lodge shall be and remain a body corporate for the term of twenty years. And for the purpose of a compliance with the Act of Congress heretofore cited, we, S. S. Davis, of New Hampshire; Joseph Dowdall, of Ohio; John B. Stumph, of Indiana, and D. B. Woodruff, of Georgia, Officers and Trustees of said Supreme Lodge, Past Supreme Chancellor, Jos. T. K. Plant, of the District of Columbia, Past Supreme Chancellor Read, of New Jersey, and Past Grand Chancellors Frederick D. Stuart, G. J. L. Foxwell, Richard Goodhart, A. T. Cavis, and A. J. Gunning, all of the District of Columbia, as incorporators, have hereunto affixed their hands and seal this Fifth day of October, A. D. 1875.

> S. S. DAVIS, S.C., SEAL.
> JOSEPH DOWDALL, S.K. of R. & S., SEAL.
> JOHN B. STUMPH, S.M. of E, SEAL.
> D. B. WOODRUFF, S.V.C., SEAL.
> SAMUEL READ, P.S.C., SEAL.
> JOS. T. K. PLANT, P.S.C., SEAL.
> FRED. D. STUART, P.G.C., SEAL.
> G. J. L. FOXWELL, P.G.C., SEAL.
> RICHARD GOODHART, P.G.C., SEAL.
> A. T. CAVIS, P.G.C., SEAL.
> A. J. GUNNING, P.G.C., SEAL.]

484.

In witness whereof, we, the undersigned officers and members of the Supreme Lodge of Knights of Pythias of the World, have hereunto affixed our hands and seals, this ...... day of August, A. D., 1870.

> JOS. T. K. PLANT, SEAL.   CLARENCE M. BARTON, SEAL.
> EDWARD DUNN, SEAL.   H. KRONHEIMER, SEAL.
> FRANCIS WOOD, SEAL.   HUGH G. DIVINE, SEAL.
> JOS. S. MARTIN, SEAL.

485.

The foregoing is the original certificate of Incorporation, with the amendments made thereto, inserted in [ ].

486.

The original certificate was acknowledged on August 5th, 1870, by the parties thereto, before R. H. Marsh, Justice of the Peace, at Washington, D. C., and recorded on the same day in the Register's Office, in Liber "Deeds of Incorporation," folio 75, D. C.

487.

The amendments were also properly acknowledged by the parties purporting to execute the same, and duly and properly recorded.

> 1876, Journal, 1201, 1266, 1293.
> 1875, Journal, 1047, 1123.
> 1874, Journal, 848, 849, 907.
> 1871, Journal, 261, 313, 341, 382, 383.

CONSTITUTION. [a]

[The original Constitutions as adopted by the Supreme Lodge, will be found as notes to this Constitution.]

1873, Journal, 753–756, 785–787.
1874, Journal, 912–914, 946, 947–965.

ARTICLE I.

SUPREME LODGE—POWERS.

488.

SECTION 1. The Supreme Lodge is the source of all true and legitimate authority in the Order of Knights of Pythias wheresoever established; it possesses original and exclusive jurisdiction and power—

489.

1. To establish, regulate and control the Forms, Ceremonies, Written and Unwritten Work, and to change, alter and annul the same, and to provide for the safe keeping and uniform teaching and dissemination of the same.

490.

2. To provide, print and furnish all Rituals, Forms, Ceremonies, Cards and Odes, Charts and Certificates.

491.

3. To prescribe the form, material and color of all Regalia, Emblems, Jewels and Charts, and to designate the Uniform of the Order.

492.

4. To provide for the emanation and distribution of all passwords, and regulate the mode and manner of using the same, and generally to prescribe such regulations as may be necessary to secure the safe and easy intercourse and identification of the brethren.

(a) Constitution of the Supreme Lodge, Knights of Pythias:

1868, Journal, 16–20, 38, 49–51, 59.

ARTICLE I.

SECTION 1. The Supreme Lodge, Knights of Pythias, is the supreme power of the Order.

SEC. 2. It is the source of all true and legitimate authority over the Order, and possesses as such supreme and absolute power over the same, and all the work belonging thereto. To it belongs the exclusive right to establish, regulate and control the Forms, Ceremonies, Written and Unwritten Work, and to change, alter and annul the same; to

8

493.

5.   To establish the Order in States, Districts, Territories, Provinces or Countries where the same has not been engrafted.

494.

6.   To provide a revenue for the Supreme Lodge by means of a representative tax on each Grand Lodge and charges for supplies furnished by it, and dues from Subordinate Lodges under its immediate jurisdiction.

495.

7.   To provide for annual returns from each Grand Lodge, and for semi-annual returns from each Subordinate Lodge under its immediate jurisdiction.

496.

8.   To hear and determine all appeals from Grand and Subordinate Lodges, when the same are properly brought before it in accordance with the regulations of the Order, and to provide by legislation for the enforcement of its decisions.

497.

9.   To enact laws and regulations of general application to carry into effect the foregoing and all other powers reserved by this Constitution to the Supreme Lodge or its officers, and such as may be necessary to enforce its legitimate authority over Grand and Subordinate Lodges under its immediate jurisdiction.

498.

10.   To charter Grand Lodges and to define the territorial extent of their jurisdiction, and to charter Subordinate Lodges not within the territorial jurisdiction of any Grand Lodge, and to provide a Constitution for each Subordinate Lodge under its immediate jurisdition.

---

provide and print all Forms, Ceremonies, Cards, Odes and Rituals, and to prescribe the style of Regalia and Emblems.

SEC. 3.   To it belongs the power to establish the Order in States, Districts, Territories, or Foreign Countries, wherein the same has not been engrafted; also to enact all laws and regulations of general application for the government of the Order, and it possesses all power and authority not expressly delegated to Grand or Subordinate Lodges by their charters or dispensations, or general laws of the Order.

SEC. 4.   To it belongs the right and power of granting charters or dispensations to Grand Lodges, and to Subordinate Lodges, in jurisdiction where no Grand Lodge exists.

ARTICLE II. (a)

HOW CONSTITUTED.

499.

SECTION 1.   The Supreme Lodge shall consist of:

1.   All Past Supreme Chancellors.
2.   Past Supreme Chancellor.
3.   Supreme Chancellor (presiding officer).
4.   Supreme Vice Chancellor.
5.   Supreme Prelate.
6.   Supreme Master of Exchequer.
7.   Supreme Keeper of Records and Seal.
8.   Supreme Master-at-Arms.
9.   Supreme Inner Guard.
10.   Supreme Outer Guard.
11.   Two Supreme Representatives from each Grand Lodge under the jurisdiction of the Supreme Lodge, until there are 20 000 members belonging to one Grand Lodge; and one Supreme Representative for each additional 10,000 members; *Provided*, That no Grand Lodge shall be entitled to more than four Supreme Representatives.

500.

SEC. 2.   Supreme Representatives must be Past Grand Chancellors in good standing in their respective Grand and

---

(a) Original Supreme Lodge Constitution:

ARTICLE II. (1) — HOW CONSTITUTED.

SECTION 1.   The Supreme Lodge shall consist of—1.   All Past Supreme Chancellors.   2.   Supreme Venerable Patriarch.   3.   Supreme Chancellor, (presiding officer.)   4.   Supreme Vice Chancellor.   5. Supreme Recording and Corresponding Scribe.   6.   Supreme Banker. 7.   Supreme Guide.   8.   Supreme Inner Steward.   9.   Supreme Outer Steward.   10.   Two Supreme Representatives from each Grand Lodge under the jurisdiction of the Supreme Lodge.

SEC. 2.   Supreme Representatives must be Past Grand Chancellors, in good standing in their respective Grand and Subordinate Lodges, and shall be elected as follows: At the next annual election after the adoption of this Article, each Grand Lodge shall elect, in the mode provided for electing Grand Lodge Officers in the Constitution of the respective Grand Lodges, two Supreme Representatives, one to serve for one year and one to serve for two years; and annually thereafter, one to serve for two year.   In the case of a vacancy in the office of

(1)   This article as it existed until amended in 1871, was as follows:
" The Supreme Lodge shall consist of Founder and Past Supreme Chancellor; Supreme Venerable Patriarch; Supreme Chancellor, (Presiding Officer;) Supreme Vice Chancellor; Supreme Recording and Corresponding Scribe; Supreme Banker; Supreme Guide; Supreme Inner Steward; Supreme Outer Steward; All Past Supreme Chancellors; All Past Grand Chancellors.   Each of the individuals above enumerated shall be entitled when present, to one vote in all the proceedings of the Supreme Lodge; three Representatives of each Grand Lodge (who shall be Past Grand Chancellors, except in cases of new Grand Lodges) that holds its Charter under the jurisdiction of the Supreme Lodge.   No person shall be eligible to any office in the Supreme Lodge, unless he shall be a Past Grand Chancellor."

1870, Journal, 192.
1871, Journal, 411-416.

Subordinate Lodges, and shall be elected as follows: At the next annual election after the adoption of this Constitution, and annually thereafter, each Grand Jurisdiction shall elect in the mode provided for electing Grand Lodge Officers in the Constitution of the respective Grand Lodges, one Supreme Representative to serve for two years; *Provided*, That each Supreme Representative now admitted shall continue in office to the expiration of his present term. In case of the vacancy in the office of the Supreme Representative, from death, removal, or any other cause, the Grand Lodge which he represented shall determine how such vacancy shall be filled. At the organization of any new Grand Lodge, two Supreme Representatives shall be elected, one to serve for one year and one to serve for two years. *And, provided further*, Where any Grand Jurisdiction is entitled, under the provisions of this Constitution, to more than two Supreme Representatives, the additional Representative or Representatives shall be elected biennially, in conformity to this Constitution, and in such a manner that if there are four Representatives, the terms of two thereof shall expire each alternate year. Each Officer and Supreme Representative shall be entitled to one vote in determining any question before the Supreme Lodge, and each Past Supreme Chancellor shall be entitled to discuss any question, but not vote.

501.

SEC. 3. All Past Grand Chancellors duly recognized by the Supreme Lodge, shall be admitted to its session and be entitled to seats therein, but shall not be entitled to speak unless by permission of the Supreme Lodge, and shall not be entitled to vote.

502.

SEC. 4. No one shall be eligible to any office in the Supreme Lodge, unless he has been duly admitted to the Supreme Lodge by being either a Representative or a Past Grand Chancellor.

---

the Supreme Representative. from death, removal, or any other cause, the Grand Lodge shall determine how such vacancy shall be filled.

SEC. 3. Each Officer and Supreme Representative shall be entitled to one vote in determining any question before the Supreme Lodge, and each Past Supreme Chancellor shall be entitled to discuss any question.

SEC. 4. All Past Grand Chancellors duly recognized by the Supreme Lodge, shall be admitted to its session and be entitled to seats therein, but shall not be entitled to speak unless by permission of the Supreme Lodge.

SEC. 5. No one shall be eligible to any office in the Supreme Lodge, unless he has been duly admitted to the Supreme Lodge, by being either a Representative or a Past Grand Chancellor.

SEC. 6. All acts inconsistent with the above, be, and are hereby repealed.

ARTICLE III. (a)

DUTIES OF OFFICERS.

503.

SECTION 1. The Past Supreme Chancellor shall have charge of and supervise the arrangement of the Altar or any other necessary floor work.

504.

SEC. 2. The Supreme Chancellor shall exercise, as occasion may require, all the rights appertaining to his high office, in accordance with the usages of the Order. He shall have a watchful supervision over all Lodges, Grand and Subordinate, and see that all the constitutional enactments, rules and edicts of the Supreme Lodge are duly and promptly observed, and that the dress, work and discipline of the Order every where are uniform.

Among his special prerogatives are the following:

505.

To call special sessions of the Supreme Lodge, or conventions of Supreme Officers in council.

506.

To visit any Grand or Subordinate Lodge under the immediate jurisdiction of this Supreme Lodge, and to give such instructions and directions as the good of the Order may require, always adhering to the obligatory usages of the Order. To cause to be executed and securely to preserve and keep the official bonds and securities of the Supreme Master of Exchequer and Supreme Keeper of Records and Seal.

(a) Original Supreme Lodge Constitution:

ARTICLE III.—DUTIES OF OFFICERS.

SECTION 1. The Supreme Venerable Patriarch shall open and close the Supreme Lodge with prayer.

SEC. 2. The Supreme Chancellor shall exercise, as occasion may require, all the rights appertaining to his high office, in accordance with the usages of the Order. He shall have a watchful supervision over all Lodges, Grand and Subordinate, and see that all the Constitutional Enactments, Rules and Edicts of the Supreme Lodge, are duly and promptly observed, and that the dress, work and discipline of the Order everywhere are uniform. Among his special prerogatives are the following: To call special sessions of the Supreme Lodge. To visit or preside at any Lodge, Grand or Subordinate, and to give such instructions and directions as the good of the Order may require, always adhering to the landmarks of the Order. To cause to be executed and securely to preserve and keep the official bonds and securities of the Supreme Banker, and Supreme Recording and Corresponding Scribe.

To grant letters of dispensation during the recess of the Supreme Lodge for the institution of new Lodges, with dispensations to be in force until charters are granted in lieu thereof, and to promptly notify the Supreme Recording and Corresponding Scribe of the issuing of said letters of dispensation. To grant dispensation during the recess

507.

To grant Warrants of Dispensation during the recess of
the Supreme Lodge for the institution of new Subordinate
Lodges, which Dispensations to be in force until taken up
by Charters granted in lieu thereof by a properly instituted
Grand Lodge, and to promptly notify the Supreme Keeper
of Records and Seal of the issuing of said Warrants of Dispensation.

508.

To grant Warrants of Dispensation during the recess of
the Supreme Lodge for the institution of Grand Lodges in
States, Countries, Districts, or Territories where the same
have not been established.

509.

To manage the contingent fund of the Supreme Lodge,
and suspend or remove any derelict or contumacious officer
for *cause*, he having right of appeal to the Supreme Lodge,
and to fill any vacancy by appointment until filled by
regular election.

510.

To appoint and commission a Deputy Supreme Chancellor
for special purposes of instituting Grand Lodges and installing their officers, or otherwise, as may be required, in all
States, Districts, Territories, or Countries, where Lodges are
established, and not having any Grand Lodge. He shall at
the next regular session present a full report of his acts
during the recess of the Supreme Lodge. He may hear and
decide such questions of law as may be submitted to him by
Grand and Subordinate Lodges under the immediate jurisdiction of this Supreme Lodge, and all such decisions shall
be binding upon the bodies submitting the same, until fully
passed upon and disaffirmed or reversed by this Supreme
Lodge.

---

of the Supreme Lodge for the institution of State Grand Lodges in
States, Districts or Territories, where the same have not been heretofore established. To manage the contingent fund of the Supreme
Lodge. To appoint a Deputy Grand Chancellor in all States, Districts,
Territories, or Foreign Countries where Lodges are established, and
not having any Grand Lodge. He shall at the annual session present
a report of his acts during the recess of the Supreme Lodge. He may
hear and decide such appeals and questions of law as may be submitted
to him by Grand and Subordinate Lodges, and all such decisions shall
be binding upon the bodies submitting the same, until reversed by
this Supreme Lodge.

Sec. 3. The Supreme Vice Chancellor, in the event of the death,
removal or physical incompetency of his superior, shall act as Supreme
Chancellor ; at all other times he shall perform such duties as may be
assigned him by the Supreme Lodge or the Supreme Chancellor.

Sec. 4. The Supreme Recording and Corresponding Scribe shall
keep a just and true record of all the proceedings of the Supreme Lodge

511.

SEC. 3. The Supreme Vice Chancellor, in the event of the death, removal or physical incompetency of his superior, shall act as Supreme Chancellor; at all other times he shall perform such duties as may be assigned him by the Supreme Lodge or the Supreme Chancellor.

512.

SEC. 4. The Supreme Prelate shall open and close the Supreme Lodge with prayer, and perform all obligatory ceremonial as prescribed in the Ritual or usages of the Order, and such other duties as comport with his office.

513.

SEC. 5. The Supreme Master of Exchequer shall render to the Supreme Chancellor a quarterly statement of the condition of funds in his hands, and make to the Supreme Lodge at its regular sessions, a true and perfect account of his doings, together with an account of all moneys received and disbursed, giving items in detail—the earnings thereon accrued from interest or other investments; to pay all orders drawn on him by the Supreme Chancellor, properly attested by the Supreme Keeper of Records and Seal. For the faithful performance of his duties he shall give bond, to be executed and approved before his installation, in the sum of ten thousand dollars, with unexceptionable securities, or otherwise the office to be declared vacant, and filled by election.

514.

SEC. 6. The Supreme Keeper of Records and Seal shall keep a just and true record of all the proceedings of the Supreme Council and Lodge at each session, and transmit

---

at each session, and transmit annually to each Grand Lodge as many copies thereof as the Lodge has Past Grand Chancellors and Officers, and two copies for each Subordinate Lodge. He shall collect all the revenues of the Supreme Lodge, and pay over the amount to the Supreme Banker, whenever it reaches the sum of $100. He shall preserve the archives, have charge of the Seal, books, papers, and other properties of the Supreme Lodge, and deliver the same to his successor, when required so to do by the Supreme Lodge. He shall prepare all charters and dispensations for Grand and Subordinate Lodges; notify officially all Grand Lodges and members of the Supreme Lodge of all sessions of the Supreme Lodge; carry on the necessary correspondence of the Lodge; keep a register which shall contain a list of all charters or dispensations granted to Grand or Subordinate Lodges, and a record of all Past Grand Chancellors and Representatives entitled to seats in the Supreme Lodge. He shall attest all official papers and documents, perform such other duties as are required by the laws and regulations of the Order, and as the Supreme Lodge may from time to time direct. He shall be furnished with an office, and shall have regular office hours, and give notice to all Grand Lodges of the time at which he will so attend, and at each annual session present a report of the general condition of the Order to the Supreme Lodge. He shall have power to

annually to each Grand Lodge as many copies thereof as the Lodge has Past Grand Chancellors and officers, and one copy for each Subordinate Lodge in their several Jurisdictions, and one to each Lodge under the immediate jurisdiction of the Supreme Lodge. He shall collect all the revenues of the Supreme Lodge, and pay over the amount to the Supreme Master of Exchequer whenever it reaches the sum of $100. He shall preserve the Archives, have charge of the Seal, Books, Papers, and other properties of the Supreme Lodge, and deliver the same to his successor when required so to do by the Supreme Lodge. He shall prepare all Charters for Grand Lodges; notify officially all Grand Lodges and officers and members of the Supreme Lodge of all sessions of the Supreme Lodge; carry on the necessary correspondence of the Lodge; keep a register which shall contain a list of all Dispensations and Charters granted to Grand, or Warrants of Dispensation issued by the Supreme Chancellor for Subordinate Lodges, and a record of all Past Grand Chancellors and Representatives entitled to seats in the Supreme Lodge. He shall attest all necesary official papers and documents, perform such other duties as are required by the laws and regulations of the Order, and as the Supreme Chancellor or Supreme Lodge may from time to time direct. He shall be furnished with an office, and shall have regular office hours, and give notice to all Grand Lodges of the time at which he will so attend, and at each session present a report of the general condition of the Order to the Supreme Lodge. He shall have power to provide himself, at the expense of the Supreme Lodge, with such books, papers and stationery as are necessary for the fulfillment of his

---

papers and stationery as are necessary for the fullfilment of his duties, provide himself, at the expense of the Supreme Lodge, with such books, and keep in his office a copy of the Seal of each Grand and Subordinate Lodge. He shall render annually to the Finance Committee, copies of his accounts with the Grand and Subordinate Lodges, etc. He shall receive for his services the sum of seven hundred and fifty dollars per annum, payable quarterly. He shall give bond in the sum of one thousand dollars for the faithful performance of his duties.

SEC. 5. The Supreme Banker shall render to the Supreme Lodge at its Annual Session, a true and perfect account of his doings, together with an account of all moneys received and disbursed—the earnings thereon accrued from investments. To pay all orders drawn on him by the Supreme Chancellor, properly attested by the S. R. and C. S. For the faithful performance of his duties he shall give bond in the sum of one thousand dollars.

SEC. 6. The duties of the Supreme Guide, Inner and Outer Stewards, are such as are traditionally appropriate to their respective stations, or such as may be assigned them by the Supreme Lodge.

SEC. 7. All Deputy Grand Chancellors (of Jurisdictions in which there are no Grand Lodges) shall install the Officers of all Subordinate Lodges within their Jurisdictions, or cause the same to be done, and perform such other duties as the Supreme Chancellor may direct.

duties, and keep in his office a copy of the Seal of each Grand and Subordinate Lodge. He shall submit a quarterly trial balance to the Supreme Chancellor for examination, as also render to each Regular Session of the Supreme Lodge. *full* and exhaustive copies of his accounts with the Grand and Subordinate Lodges, etc., of and during the *whole* term of recess passed. He shall receive for his services the sum of one thousand dollars per annum, * payable quarterly. For the faithful performance of his duties he shall give bond, to be executed and approved before his installation, in the sum of ten thousand dollars, with unexceptionable securities, or otherwise the office to be declared vacant, and filled by election.

* 1875, Journal, 1168. 1876, Journal, 1324, 1329.

515.

SEC. 7. The duties of the Supreme Master-at-Arms, Inner and Outer Guards are such as are traditionally appropriate to their respective stations, or such as may be assigned them by the Supreme Lodge.

516.

SEC. 8. All Deputy Supreme Chancellors (of Jurisdictions in which there are no Grand Lodges) shall install the Officers of all Subordinate Lodges within their Jurisdictions, or cause the same to be done, and perform such other duties as the Supreme Chancellor may direct.

ARTICLE IV. (a)

SESSIONS.

517.

Sessions of the Supreme Lodge shall be held annually, at such time in the months of April, May, June, July or August, as the Supreme Lodge may at each Annual Session determine; *Provided*, That if the Supreme Lodge neglects to fix any special time it shall convene on the third Tuesday of April.

518.

The place for the holding of each Annual Session shall be fixed at the preceding Annual Session; *Provided*, That if no place is fixed by the Supreme Lodge, the Annual Session shall be held in the city of Baltimore.

(a) Original Supreme Lodge Constitution:

ARTICLE IV. (1) — SESSIONS.

The meetings shall be held annually on the Third Tuesday in April, at such place as may be agreed upon by a majority of votes at a regular annual session.

(1) This Article, until amended in 1870, read "Second Tuesday in March," in place of "Third Tuesday in April."

1870, Journal, 165, 228.

ARTICLE V. (a)

COMMITTEES.

519.

SECTION 1. The following Committees shall be appointed annually by the Supreme Chancellor:
Committee on Law and Supervision.
Committee on Finance.
Committee on Appeals and Grievances.
Committee on Credentials and Returns.
Committee on Mileage.
Committee on State of the Order.
Committee on Written Work.
Committee on Unwritten Work.
Committee on Printing.
Committee on Dispensations and Charters.

520.

SEC. 2. The Committee on Law and Supervision shall, when such subjects are presented to the Supreme Lodge and duly referred to them, inquire into all cases of infraction of the established laws and regulations of the Order, and recommend such measures as they may deem expedient for correcting the innovation, and further consider and have charge of all matters coming within the purview of that Committee.

521.

SEC. 3. The Committee on Finance shall examine the accounts of the Supreme Master of Exchequer and Supreme Keeper of Records and Seal, at each Session, and whenever required so to do by the Supreme Lodge. They shall examine and pass upon all bills presented to the Supreme Lodge when in session, and, if correct, report, if approving the same, for economy or creating a remedy by legislation for all extravagant expenditures. They shall make estimates for and

---

(a) Original Supreme Lodge Constitution:

ARTICLE V.—COMMITTEES.

SEC. 1. The following Committees shall be appointed annually by the Supreme Chancellor:
Committee on Laws and Supervision.
Committee on Finance and Mileage.
Committee on Appeals and Grievances.
Committee on Returns and Credentials.
SEC. 2. The Committee on Laws and Supervision (1) shall, when such subjects are presented to the Supreme Lodge and duly referred

---

(1) This Section until amended in 1871, contained between the words "Supervision" and "shall" these additional words: "shall examine the Constitution, General Laws and By-Laws of Grand Lodges, and all By-Laws of Subordinate Lodges (where there are no Grand Lodges) under its Jurisdiction, before being printed; correct any article or section which may conflict with the Constitution and General Laws of the Supreme Lodge. They"

recommend appropriations of moneys for general or specific purposes during recess of the Supreme Lodge, and bring down an approximate estimate, based on past results, of the probable revenue likely to accrue ; and no expenditures of any character shall be made in excess of the appropriation then made until the next Regular Session.

522.

Sec. 4. The Committee on Appeals and Grievances shall hear all appeals and grievances from Grand Lodges or members of Lodges referred to them by the Supreme Lodge, or Supreme Chancellor, and report thereon with the utmost dispatch.

523.

Sec. 5. The Committee on Credentials and Returns shall examine and report on the returns of the Grand Lodges and Subordinate under the immediate jurisdiction of the Supreme Lodge, and the Credentials of all Past Grand Chancellors and Representatives to the Supreme Lodge.

524.

Sec. 6. The Committee on Mileage shall compute the mileage and per diem of all Supreme Officers and Representatives, at each Regular or Special called Session, making out a proper, complete and accurate roll of the same, and report the amount to which each one on the roll is entitled; and no order shall be drawn for the same until said report is indorsed by a majority of the Committee.

525.

Sec. 7. The Committee on the State of the Order shall examine and report upon such portions of reports of the Supreme Officers and D. S. Cs., so far as the same relate to the state of the Order, and upon such other matters as may be referred to them, presenting in their reports an exhibit of

---

to them, inquire into all cases of infraction of the established laws and regulations of the Order, and recommend such measures as they may deem expedient for correcting the innovations.

Sec. 3. The Committee on Finance and Mileage shall examine the accounts of the Supreme Banker and S. R. and C. S., at each annual session, and whenever required so to do by the Supreme Lodge. They shall examine all bills presented to the Supreme Lodge, and when correct, report the same for payment. They shall compute the mileage of Officers and Representatives, and report the amount to which each is entitled; and no order shall be drawn for such amount until the bill for the same is endorsed by a majority of the Committee.

Sec. 4. The Committee on Appeals and Grievances shall hear all appeals and grievances, from Grand Lodges or members of Lodges,

the condition and progress of the Order, and recommending such measures for the good and prosperity of the whole Order as they may think the circumstances require.

526.

SEC. 8. The Committee on Written work shall examine and report upon such parts of reports of the Supreme Officers or other matters referred to them pertaining to all Written Work of the Order of a public nature, covering Regalias, Jewels, Charts, Certificates, Shields, Uniforms, Equipments or Public Ceremonials, Forms for and details of matters not properly of a secret nature.

527.

SEC. 9. The Committee on Unwritten Work shall examine and report upon such reports of the Supreme Officers or other matters referred to them of a nature that may be strictly private, or in consonance and keeping with the duties of the name of the Committee.

523.

SEC. 10. The Committee on Printing shall have general supervisory charge of and examine into all matters referred to or coming within the purview of their duties as suggested by their name; make all contracts not otherwise provided for, compare materials, qualities and price, analyze all bills submitted for printing, binding and supplies, establish a standard style, quality and grade of same, and report their findings and recommendations to the Supreme Lodge.

529.

SEC. 11. The Committee on Dispensations and Charters shall examine into all proper matters referred to them from the Supreme Officers' reports; they shall examine and report on all petitions for Warrants of Dispensation issued by the Supreme Chancellor for Subordinate or Grand Lodges, or applications for Charters for the same, approving or disapproving of the issuing of the same, and other general Dispensations, or D. S. C's Commissions issued during the recess of the Supreme Lodge.

---

referred to them by the Supreme Lodge or Supreme Chancellor, and report thereon with the utmost dispatch.

SEC. 5. The Committee on Returns and Credentials shall examine the returns of the Grand Lodges and Subordinate Lodges not working under the control of a State Grand Lodge, and the Credentials of all Past Grand Chancellors and Representatives to the Supreme Lodge.

SEC. 6. Each of the above named Committees shall consist of three members, and when serving on actual work during a recess shall have their necessary expenses paid.

530.

· Sec. 12. Each of the above named Committees shall consist of five (a) members, and when serving on actual work during a recess, by order of the Supreme Lodge or of the Supreme Chancellor, shall have their necessary expenses paid.

ARTICLE VI. (b)
MODE OF FORMING A GRAND LODGE.

531.

Section 1. All Subordinate Lodges in Jurisdictions where no Grand Lodge exists, shall be under the immediate control of this Supreme Lodge until the formation of a Grand Lodge for that Jurisdiction. and shall pay to the Supreme Lodge, while under its control, fifty cents per capita tax on each member annually.

532.

Sec. 2. When there are five or more Subordinate Lodges established and in working order in any Jurisdiction, they, through the Deputy Supreme Chancellor thereof, may petition the Supreme Chancellor, who shall cause the Supreme Keeper of Records and Seal to notify each of the Lodges of

---

(a) Until amended in 1876, this Section read "three," in place of "five."—1875, Journal, 1168. 1876, Journal, 1325, 1329.

(b) Original Supreme Lodge Constitution:

ARTICLE VI.—Mode of Forming a Grand Lodge.

Sec. 1. All Subordinate Lodges in jurisdictions where no Grand Lodge exists, shall be under the immediate control of this Supreme Lodge, until the formation of a Grand Lodge of that Jurisdiction, and shall pay to the Supreme Lodge, while under its control, five per cent. on its gross receipts semi-annually.

Sec. 2. When there are five Subordinate Lodges established and in working order in any Jurisdiction, the Deputy Grand Chancellor thereof shall notify the Supreme Chancellor, who shall cause the Supreme Recording and Corresponding Scribe to notify the Lodges of that Jurisdiction to elect *three Representatives for one year*, on the first meeting night after the receipt of the communication.

Sec. 3. The Past Chancellors of the five Lodges, together with the Representatives elect, shall meet at such place as may be specified by the Supreme Chancellor, and proceed to organize a Grand Lodge by electing a V.G.P., G.C., V.G.C., G.R. and C.S., G.B., G.G., G.I.S. and G.O.S., and three (1) Representatives to the Supreme Lodge, all of whom must be Past Chancellors.

Sec. 4. A notice of their organization, together with a list of their officers, shall be forwarded to the Supreme R. and C. Scribe through the Supreme Chancellor, and the latter officer shall install, or cause to be installed, the officers elect of said Grand Lodge, after which it shall proceed to frame By-Laws for its own government, no inconsistent with the laws promulgated by this Body.

---

(1) This provision was not in terms amended, but was so in effect, by the amendment made to Article II ante, made in 1870. See also as bearing on same subject Section 2, Article VII of Grand Lodge Constitution, note, page 112, post.

that Juris diction to elect two Representatives for the unexpired balance of the year, up to the 31st day of December following, on the first meeting night of the Lodge after the receipt of the communication.

533.

SEC. 3.   The Past Chancellors of the five or more Lodges, together with the Representatives elect, shall meet at such place as may be specified by the Supreme Chancellor, and proceed to organize a Grand Lodge by electing a Past Grand Chancellor, Grand Chancellor, Grand Vice Chancellor, Grand Prelate, Grand Master of Exchequer, Grand Keeper of Records and Seal, Grand Master-at-Arms, Grand Inner Guard, Grand Outer Guard, all of whom must be Past Chancellors.

534.

SEC. 4.   The Grand Lodge, as soon as organized, shall elect two Representatives to the Supreme Lodge, as prescribed in Section 2, Art. II of the Constitution, and the said Representatives are hereby declared Past Grand Chancellors.

535.

SEC. 5.   A notice of their organization, together with a list of their officers shall be forwarded to the Supreme K. of R. and S. through the Supreme Chancellor, and the latter officer shall install, or cause to be installed, by a Deputy Supreme Chancellor, the officers elect of said Grand Lodge, after which it shall proceed to frame a Constitution and By-Laws for its own government, not inconsistent with the laws promulgated by this Body.

ARTICLE VII. (a)

OF GRAND LODGE.

536.

SECTION 1.   Grand Lodges exist by virtue of a Charter or Dispensation issued by authority of the Supreme Lodge, or Supreme Chancellor during its recess.   They shall conform

---

(a)   Constitution for Grand Lodges:
1868, Journal, 16-20, 38, 52, 53, 59.

☞ (All matter *italicised* is of general application and obligatory ; all matter not italicised is recommendatory.)

ARTICLE I.

This body shall be known as the Grand Lodge of Knights of Pythias of the State of ....

ARTICLE II.—COMPOSITION.

It shall be composed of all Past Chancellors of Subordinate Lodges in the State.

CONSTITUTION. 109

to the Ritual, Forms, Ceremonies, Work, Regalia, Jewels, Uniform, Charts, Shields and Certificates, and regulations prescribed by the Supreme Lodge, in accordance with this Constitution, and shall (subject to the provisions hereof and right of appeal) have exclusive original jurisdiction over all Subordinate Lodges within their territorial limit, and over the members attached to the same.

537.

Sec. 2. All power and authority not herein reserved to the Supreme Lodge, is hereby delegated to the Grand Lodges; the Supreme Lodge, however, reserving to itself the right

ARTICLE III.—Jurisdiction.

This Grand Lodge shall have jurisdiction over all Lodges of Knights of Pythias within the State of .... It possesses the right and power of granting Charters, of suspending or taking away the same upon proper cause, of receiving and hearing all appeals, of redressing grievances and complaints arising in the Lodges under its jurisdiction, of enacting By-Laws for its government and support, provided the same are not in violation of the laws of the Supreme Lodge.

ARTICLE IV.—Qualification of Members.

Every member of, and Representative to the Grand Lodge, must be regular contributing members in good standing of a Subordinate Lodge.

ARTICLE V.—Sessions.

Section 1. This Grand Lodge shall hold an annual session on the ...... day of January, and may hold (1) a semi-annual session on the ...... day of July. The hour and place of meeting shall be fixed as the Grand Lodge may determine.

Sec. 2. At the session of July, if any be held at that time (2), the returns of the Subordinate Lodges for the previous six months will be received, and nominations made for officers for the ensuing year, and such other business transacted as may come legally before the Grand Lodge.

Sec. 3. At the annual session in January, the returns for the previous six months, will be received, the officers of the Grand Lodge, for the ensuing year, elected and installed, and such other business transacted as may be determined upon.

ARTICLE VI.—Officers.

Sec. 1. *The elective officers shall be the G.C., V.G.C., G.R. and C.S. and G.B., and Grand Representatives to the Supreme Lodge.*

The appointive officers shall be the Grand Guide, Grand Inner and Outer Stewards, the District Deputy Grand Chancellors. The retiring Grand Chancellor shall fill the office of Venerable Grand Patriarch.

Sec. 2. The Grand Chancellor shall preside at all sessions of the Grand Lodge, enforce order and decorum; decide all questions of order without debate, subject, however, to an appeal to the Grand Lodge by two members; appoint Grand Officers, *pro tem,* in case of

(1) The words "may hold" inserted by amendment of 1870. 1870, Journal, 188, 202

(2) The words "if any be held at that time" inserted by amendment of 1870. 1870, Journal, 188, 202.

at any time, by proper amendments, duly adopted, to this Constitution, to resume any additional power necessary to promote the well-being and harmony of the Order.

538.

SEC. 3.   Each Grand Lodge shall adopt a Constitution for its own government, and also a Constitution for its Subordinates, which Constitutions shall be in accordance with the provisions of this Constitution and the laws made in pursuance hereof.   The Constitutions of Grand Lodges, and all

---

temporary absence or disqualification of any Grand Officer; appoint all committees, unless otherwise ordered; sign all orders drawn on the Grand Banker, for such sums as may be voted by the Grand Lodge, and such other papers as may require his signature to authenticate them; exercise a general supervision over the Order in this Jurisdition. He shall call the Vice Grand Chancellor to his chair during the discussion of any question before the Grand Lodge on which he may desire to speak. He shall, on the day of his installation, appoint the following committees to serve for the term of one year, to wit: A Committee on Laws and Supervision. A Committee on Finance and Mileage. A Committee on Appeals and Grievances. A Committee on Returns and Credentials. He shall, at each stated session, present and cause to be read to this Grand Lodge, his semi-annual report. He shall visit, officially, at least once during his term of office, accompanied by such of his Grand Officers as he may select, each Subordinate Lodge in the district in which he resides. All necessary reasonable expenses, incurred on such visits, shall be paid by this Grand Lodge.

SEC. 3. The Vice Grand Chancellor is the counsellor and assistant of the Grand Chancellor. In the absence of the Grand Chancellor he shall preside over the Grand Lodge. In case of the removal, death, resignation, or inability of the Grand Chancellor, the powers of said officer shall devolve on the Vice Grand Chancellor for the time being.

SEC. 4. The Grand Recording and Corresponding Scribe shall keep a just and true record of all the proceedings of the Grand Lodge at each session, and transmit annually to each Subordinate Lodge, as many copies thereof as the Lodge has Past Chancellors and Officers; preserve the archives, have charge of the seal, books, papers and other properties of the Grand Lodge, and deliver the same to his successor when required so to do by the Grand Lodge; prepare all Charters and Dispensations for Subordinate Lodges; notify officially all Subordinate Lodges within the State of all meetings of the Grand Lodge; carry on the necessary correspondence of the Grand Lodge; keep a register, which shall contain a list of all charters granted to Subordinate Lodges, and a record of all Past Chancellors and Representatives entitled to seats in this Grand Lodge; also keep a record and notify all Subordinate Lodges on the receipt of such information, of all rejected candidates and suspended members; attest all official papers and documents; perform such other duties as are required by the Laws and Regulation of the Order, and as the Grand Lodge may from time to time direct. Have his regular office hours, and give notice to the Subordinate Lodges of the time at which he so will attend, and at each annual session, present a report of the general condition of the Order, to this Grand Lodge. He shall have power to provide himself, at the expense of the Grand Lodge, with such books, papers and stationery as are necessary for the fulfillment of his duties; and keep in his office a copy of the Seal of each Subordinate Lodge in his Jurisdiction.

amendments thereof, shall not go into effect until submitted to and approved by the Supreme Chancellor or Supreme Lodge.

539.

SEC. 4. Grand Lodges shall be composed only of Past Chancellors, but said Grand Lodges may provide for a representative system, and may limit the rights and privileges of Past Chancellors on the floor of the Grand Lodge.

He shall receive all moneys due to the Grand Lodge, and pay them over immediately to the Grand Banker, taking his receipt therefor, and keep an exact and true account of the same, draw all orders on the Grand Banker for such moneys as may be voted by the Grand Lodge, and attest the same; report in writing at the annual session, and at other times when so required by the Grand Lodge, the condition of the funds of the Grand Lodge, and of the accounts of Subordinate Lodges, and deliver the books to the Finance Committee whenever they may demand them. For the faithful performance of his duties, he shall receive the sum of — dollars per annum.

SEC. 5. The Grand Banker shall receive all funds for the use of the Grand Lodge from the Grand Recording and Corresponding Scribe, giving to him a receipt for the same; pay all orders drawn on him by the Grand Chancellor, properly attested; keep the accounts in a proper manner, exhibiting the sources and amounts of receipts, and the purposes and amounts of disbursements, and give a statement in writing thereof, at the stated session, or whenever required to do so by the Grand Lodge. At the expiration of his term of office, he shall deliver all books, papers and moneys (belonging to the Grand Lodge, in his possession) to his successor. Before entering upon the duties of his office, he shall give such security for the faithful performance of his trust, as the Grand Lodge may deem satisfactory, and deliver the books to the Finance Committee for examination whenever they may demand them.

SEC. 6. The Grand Guide shall assist in the ceremonies of the Grand Lodge, and in preserving order therein, examine and conduct new members and Representatives in the Grand Lodge, and execute the commands of the Grand Chancellor.

SEC. 7. The Grand Inner Steward shall have charge of the inner door. He shall see that all members of the Grand Lodge are clothed in appropriate regalia before entering the Lodge room.

SEC. 8. The Grand Outer Steward shall have charge of the outer door, allow no person to enter the anteroom without the Password, unless ordered so to do by the Grand Chancellor, and be responsible, for the safe-keeping of all regalias, jewels and other property of the Grand Lodge, while that body is in session. For the faithful performance of his duties he shall receive not less than — dollars per annum.

SEC. 9. The Representatives to the Supreme Lodge shall attend all meetings of that Body, and faithfully represent the views and interests of this Grand Lodge therein. They shall be furnished with certificates of election in such form as may be prescribed.

SEC. 10. The D.D. Grand Chancellor is the Representative of the Grand Chancellor in the district placed under his jurisdiction, and it shall be his duty to see that the work of the Order is performed uniformly; to install or cause to be installed, the officers of the Lodges under his charge, and report his doings to the Grand Chancellor in

540.

SEC. 5. The officers of a Grand Lodge shall be as prescribed in Section 3, Article VI of this Constitution, who shall be elected or appointed as the Constitutions of the respective Grand Lodges may prescribe, and who shall hold office for the term of one year.

---

time for the sessions of the Grand Lodge. He shall receive the dues and quarterly reports from the Lodges in his district, and transmit them to the Grand Recording and Corresponding Scribe within one week after the installation of officers of Subordinate Lodges. He shall receive from the Grand Recording and Corresponding Scribe, all dispensations for new Lodges under his jurisdiction, after they may have been granted by this Grand Lodge or the Grand Officers, and with the assistance of such brethren as he may deem qualified, open such new Lodges, deliver the dispensations and install the officers. He shall, when visiting Subordinate Lodges in his district, be provided with his commission, to be delivered to him by the Grand Chancellor on his appointment. He shall also perform such other duties as the Grand Lodge or the Grand Chancellor may from time to time order and direct. All necessary and reasonable expenses of the D.D. Grand Chancellor shall be paid by the Grand Lodge.

ARTICLE VII.—MODE OF ELECTION OF GRAND OFFICERS.

SEC. 1. Each Grand Lodge shall regulate the manner of electing its officers. The Grand Lodge shall pay the mileage and necessary expenses of its Officers and Representatives. The rate shall be — cents per mile.

SEC. 2. The Representatives to the Supreme Lodge must be elected for two years and must be Past Grand Chancellors. In case of new Grand Lodges the V.G.P., G.C. and V.G.C. shall, by virtue of their offices, become Past Grand Chancellors and Representatives to the Supreme Lodge, provided, however, that they shall serve out their term of office in the Grand Lodge for which they were elected.(1)

SEC. 3. The installation shall take place immediately after the result of the election is announced.

ARTICLE IX.—RETURNS AND DUES OF SUBORDINATES.

At the end of each term, each Subordinate Lodge shall pay to the Grand Lodge as dues, not less than — cents, per capita tax for every Knight in good standing, the number of which shall be shown upon the report. They shall also return the blank furnished by the Grand Lodge, properly filled out, with the signature of the C.C. and K. of R. and S. attached, and an impression of the Seal upon it.

ARTICLE XI.—QUORUM AND VOTING.

SEC. 1. In all cases where the number of Lodges in a jurisdiction exceeds 100, one-third of the Lodges, if represented, shall constitute a quorum. A majority of the Lodges shall constitute a quorum in all other cases.

SEC. 2. Each Grand Lodge shall regulate its manner of voting.

---

(1) See Sec. 3, Article VI, Supreme Lodge Constitution, ante, page 108.

541.

SEC. 6. Charters of Grand Lodges may be revoked, and Grand Lodges suspended, by the Supreme Lodge, for nonconformity to the Work, Ceremonies or Ritual adopted by the Supreme Lodge; for disobedience to its legal mandates, and for improper conduct.

ARTICLE XII.—REVENUE.

Each Grand Lodge shall regulate the price of charters or dispensations, rituals, installation work, odes and withdrawal cards. The four last named articles must, in all cases, be procured from the Supreme Lodge. In no case shall the price of charters be less than $15.

ARTICLE XIII.—DISPENSATIONS.

Dispensations can be granted by the Grand Chancellor or his Deputy upon application from a Lodge, for the following purposes:
To propose, elect and initiate at the same session.
To confer the three degrees at the same session.
To confer the degrees upon a person over fifty years of age.

ARTICLE XIV.—BY-LAWS, RULES OF ORDER AND ORDER OF BUSINESS

Each Grand Lodge shall regulate its Order of Business, and shall form its own By-Laws provided they are not in violation of this Constitution.
For the Rules of Order, "Cushing's Manual" shall be the guide.

ARTICLE XV.—BLANKS.

The following blanks will be furnished by the Grand Recording and Corresponding Scribe:
Blank semi-annual Returns.
Blank Past Chancellor's Certificate.
Blank Representative Certificate.
Blank Dispensation.
Blank District Deputy Grand Chancellor's Commission.
Blank Form of Application for Charter.

ARTICLE XVI.

Each Grand Lodge shall regulate the mode of Election for Officers in Subordinate Lodges and the mode of balloting; establish the duties of Subordinate Lodge Officers; establish the mode of conducting charges and trials.

ARTICLE VIII. [a]

OF SUBORDINATE LODGES.

542.

SECTION 1.   Subordinate Lodges exist by virtue of Dispensations issued by the Supreme Lodge through the Supreme Chancellor, or Charters granted in lieu thereof, or directly, by the appropriate Grand Lodge; but to each Grand Lodge when formed, belongs the exclusive right to issue Charters to Lodges instituted within its prescribed territorial Jurisdiction.

543.

SEC. 2.   Grand Lodges shall prescribe a Constitution for the Subordinate Lodges within their jurisdiction, but the following obligatory general rules or principles shall be incorporated into each Subordinate Lodge Constitution:

544.

1.   A Lodge shall never consist of less than seven members of the Knight Rank, and shall hold stated meetings at least once a week, at such an hour as may from time to time be determined upon; *Provided*, That each Grand Lodge may allow meeting at longer intervals by a regular dispensation.

545.

2.   Not less than seven members of the Knight Rank shall constitute a quorum for the transaction of business, including one qualified to preside, and if seven members only be present, no appropriation of money shall be made unless it be by unanimous consent.   .

(a) Constitution for Subordinate Lodges.

1868, Journal, 16–20, 39, 53–55, 59.

The italicised portions of the Constitution are obligatory, and apply to all Subordinate Lodges.

SEC. 1.   *A Lodge shall never consist of less than nine members of the Knight's Rank, including one qualified to preside, and shall hold stated meetings at least once a week, at such an hour as may from time to time be determined upon.*

SEC. 2.   *Not less than seven (1) members shall constitute a quorum for the transaction of business, and if seven (1) members only be present, no appropriations of money shall be made, unless it be by a unanimous consent.*

SEC. 3.   Special meetings may be held at such times as the business of the Lodge may require, but they shall be confined to the business that they were called to consider.   The C.C. (2) may call such meetings at his own discretion, and also when requested so to do in writing by five members of the Lodge.

---

(1) This was originally "niue" in place of "seven," until 1871.

1871, Journal, 363, 393.

(2) This was originally "W.C." in place of "C.C.," until 1872.

1872, Journal, 560, 601, 656–659.

546.

3. The Lodge shall transact all its business in the Knight Rank, except the actual conferring of the Page or Esquire Rank.

547.

4. The officers of a Subordinate Lodge shall be as provided in the Ritual of the Order.

548.

5. Nominations for the elective officers may be made on the night preceding and on the night of election.

549.

6. Officers shall be installed at the first regular meeting in the new term, if unforeseen circumstances do not prevent; but no officer shall be installed unless he has fully paid to his Lodge the amount of all dues and claims of whatsoever nature then accrued.

550.

7. All vacancies by death, removal, suspension, resignation or otherwise, shall be filled in the manner of the original selection, to serve the residue of the term, and officers so serving shall be entitled to the honors of the term.

551.

8. No person shall be initiated into a Lodge of this Order, who has not reached the legal age of majority in the country where the Lodge is located, nor unless he be a white male, of good moral character, sound in health, and a be-

---

SEC. 4. Every Lodge shall be opened at the appointed time; and in the absence of the C.C. (1) the V.C. shall preside; and in the absence of both, the senior P.C.; and if no P.C. present, a Knight may be called to the Chair by a majority of the members present.

SEC. 5. *The Lodge shall transact its actual business in the Knights' Rank.*

ARTICLE II.—Officers.

(2) SEC. 1. *The elective officers of this Lodge shall be the C.C. and V.C. and Prelate, who shall be elected semi-annually, in June and December; and the Keeper of Records and Seal, Master of Finance and Master of Exchequer, who shall be elected annually by ballot, at the last meeting of December. The retiring C.C. shall fill the office of Past Chancellor.*

---

(1) This was originally "W. C." in place of "C. C.," until 1872.
1872, Journal, 560, 601, 656–659.

(2) Until 1872 this Section was the same as above, except that "C.C.," wherever occurring, was "W.C." The words, "and Prelate" were not therein, and "Keeper of Records Seal, Master of Finance and Master of Exchequer," read "Recording Scribe, Financial Scribe and Banker."
1872, Journal, 560, 601, 656–659.

liever in a Supreme Being. Every application for membership must be accompanied with the initiation fee, the amount of which shall be fixed by each Grand Lodge ; *Provided*, That in no case shall the three ranks be conferred in North America for a less amount than ten dollars ; *Provided, further*, That the Supreme Chancellor be and he is hereby authorized and empowered, upon the application of a Grand Lodge, through its proper officers, to issue his Dispensation, authorizing and permitting such Jurisdiction to confer the three Ranks of the Order for a sum not less than six dollars.(a)

552.

9. Applications for initiation must be signed by the petitioner, stating his age, residence and occupation, and indorsed by two Knights in good standing, who are members of the Lodge, which must be entered on the records, and the petition referred to a committee of three for investigation, (neither of whom shall have recommended him,) whose duty it shall be to report on the character and qualifications of the petitioner at a regular meeting. The applicant shall then be balloted for, by secret ball ballot, and, if approved, he may be admitted.

553.

10. Should two black balls appear against a candidate, the ballot shall be renewed immediately. Should two or

---

(1) SEC. 2. *The appointive officers shall be the Master at Arms, Inner Guard and Outer Guard, who shall be appointed by the newly elected C.C. on the night of his installation.*

SEC. 3. *Any Knight in good standing having served one full term in an appointive office, shall be eligible to the office of V.C.*

SEC. 4. *Nominations for all the above elective officers shall be made on the night preceding and on the night of election, except to fill a vacancy.*

SEC. 5. *Officers shall be installed at the first regular meeting in the new term, if unforeseen circumstances do not prevent it. But no member shall be installed who is indebted to the Lodge, nor shall any officer who has been installed retain his seat if he shall be in arrears to the amount of six months' dues.*

SEC. 6. *All vacancies shall be filled in the manner of the original selection, to serve the residue of the term, and officers so serving shall be entitled to the honors of the term.*

ARTICLE III.—MODE OF ELECTION.

The Grand Lodge shall regulate the mode of election for officer or officers.

(a) This last proviso was added by the amendment made in 1876.

1875, Journal, 1168.
1876, Journal, 1325, 1330.

---

(1) This Section was as above until 1872 except that "Master at Arms, Inner Guard and Outer Guard," read "Guide, Inner and Outer Steward," and "C.C." read "W.C."

1872, Journal, 560, 601, 656–659.

more appear on the second ballot, he shall be declared rejected, and no other ballot shall be taken in his case for the space of six months thereafter.

554.

11.   One week must elapse between the conferring of the Ranks *in all cases*, except the first four meetings of a new Lodge : but in *every* instance one week must elapse between the application and the conferring of the initiatory Rank of Page.

(The above paragraph shall not apply to cases where Dispensations are granted by a proper Grand Officer, or through his Deputy.)

555.

12.   Any Brother of the Order, in good standing, desirous of becoming a member of a Lodge, shall make application as in the case of an uninitiated person, and accompany same with his withdrawal card from the Lodge of which he was last a member, or the card granted by the Grand Lodge in lieu thereof, which shall be referred to a committee of three, whose duty it shall be to report as to the standing and qualifications of the applicant at a regular meeting. The Brother shall then be balloted for by secret ball ballot, as in the case of an initiate.   Any Brother who may have lost his card can have the same renewed by applying to the source from which it emanated.

ARTICLE IV.—Voting.

The G. L. shall determine the manner of voting.

ARTICLE V.—Membership and Degrees.

SEC. 1.   *No person shall be initiated into a Lodge who is under twenty-one, or over fifty years of age, (unless by dispensation,) nor unless he be a white male citizen of good moral character, sound in health and a believer in the Supreme Being.   Every application for membership must be accompanied with the initiation fee, the amount of which shall not be less than four dollars. The fee for the Rank of Esquire shall never be less than three dollars, and the fee for the Rank of Knight shall never be less than three dollars.   The initiation fee shall in all cases accompany the application.*

SEC. 2.   *Applications for initiation must be signed by the petitioner, stating his age, residence and occupation, and endorsed by two Knights in good standing, who are members of the Lodge, which must be entered on the records, and the petition referred to a committee of three for investigation, (neither of whom shall have recommended him,) whose duty it shall be to report on the character and qualifications of the petitioner at the next regular meeting.   The applicant shall then be balloted for, and if approved, he may be admitted.*

SEC. 3.   *Should two black balls appear against a candidate, the ballot shall be renewed immediately.   Should two or more appear on the second ballot, he shall be declared rejected, and no other ballot shall be taken in his case for the space of six months thereafter.*

SEC. 4.   *One week must elapse between the conferring of the degrees, in all cases, except the first four meeting nights of a new Lodge ; but in all cases*

556.

13. No proposition for membership shall be withdrawn, unless by consent of the Lodge, after it has been referred to a committee, and all cases so referred shall be balloted for upon the report of the committee, whether it be favorable or unfavorable.

557.

14. A candidate for membership, residing in a jurisdiction other than the one in which his proposition is offered, shall not be initiated without the written consent of the Lodge nearest his residence.

558.

15. No Rank shall be conferred on a Brother who is a non-resident of the Jurisdiction, or who is a member of another Lodge, without first obtaining the permission of the Lodge to which the Brother is attached.

559.

16. No Rank shall be conferred under any pretense whatever, unless the same shall have been previously paid for

---

one week must elapse between the application and the conferring of the initiatory Rank of Page.

(*The above section shall not apply to cases where dispensations are granted.*)

SEC. 5. *Any brother of the Order, in good standing, desirous of becoming a member of a Lodge, shall send his withdrawal card from the Lodge of which he was last a member, or the card granted by the Grand Lodge in lieu thereof, which shall be referred to a committee of three, whose duty it shall be to report as to the standing and qualifications of the applicant at the next regular meeting. The brother shall then be balloted for, and if he receives a two-thirds vote of the members present, he shall be declared elected. Any brother who may have lost his card, or which may be out of date, can have the same renewed by applying to the source from which it emanated.*

SEC. 6. *No proposition for membership shall be withdrawn after it has been referred to a committee, except by unanimous consent, and all whose cases are so referred shall be balloted for upon the report of the committee, whether it be favorable or unfavorable.*

(1) SEC. 7. When an applicant for membership has been rejected, notice of his rejection shall be immediately sent by the Keeper of Records and Seal to the Grand Recording and Corresponding Scribe of the Jurisdiction; and the amount accompanying his application be returned to him by the K. of R. and S. with a notice of his rejection.

SEC. 8. Every applicant elected to membership failing to present himself for initiation or admission within six stated meetings of the Lodge after being notified of his election, (unless prevented by sickness or some other unavoidable occurrence,) shall forfeit the amount that has been paid by him to the Lodge.

SEC. 9. *No Rank shall be conferred on a brother who is a member of another Lodge, without first obtaining the permission of the Lodge to which the brother is attached.*

SEC. 10. *No Rank shall be conferred under any pretense whatever, unless the same shall have been previously paid for.*

---

(1) This section was as above until 1872, except that "Keeper of Records and Seal" wherever occurring read "Recording Scribe."

560.

17. Applications for Withdrawal Cards shall be made, either personally or in writing, to a Lodge, and a card thereupon shall be granted; *Provided*, the Brother be clear of the books, free from charges made or pending, and there be no other valid objection.

561.

18. Any Withdrawal Card may be revoked by a Lodge granting the same, or ordered vacated by the proper Grand Lodge, or Grand Chancellor, at any time, for cause appearing, and when so revoked for the purpose of impeachment or trial, the person holding said card shall again become subject to the Lodge which issued same, in so far as concerns said impeachment or trial. Refusal to comply with proper citation in this connection shall constitute contempt.

562.

19. A withdrawal card can be renewed if lost or destroyed accidentally, and satisfactory evidence adduced from the holder and applicant, by the Lodge having granted the same, and upon such terms as the Lodge may determine.

ARTICLE VI.—Cards. (1)

Applications for Withdrawal Cards shall be made either personally or in writing to a Lodge, and a card thereupon shall be granted; provided, the brother be clear of the books, and there be no valid objection. No visiting cards shall be permitted in the Order. Any withdrawal card may be revoked by a Lodge granting the same, at any time, for cause appearing.

ARTICLE VII.—Seal.

Each Lodge shall have a seal with appropriate devices, which shall be affixed to such cards, as well as to all official communications emanating from the Lodge.

ARTICLE VIII.—Duties of Officers.

The Grand Lodge shall prescribe the duties of officers.

ARTICLE IX.—Dues and Benefits. (2)

Each Subordinate Lodge shall regulate its dues and benefits; provided, however, that a member who is one year in arrears shall stand suspended.

ARTICLE X.—Charges, Trials, Etc.

The Grand Lodge shall regulate the mode of charges and trials.

---

(1) This article was as above until 1872, except the last clause, as to revoking cards, which was added that year.

1872, Journal, 335, 586.

(2) This Article as it read until 1871 was " six months " in place of " one year "

1871, Journal, 389, 417.

563.

20. Each Lodge shall have a seal with appropriate devices, which shall be affixed to such cards, as well as to all official documents emanating from the Lodge.

564.

21. A member who is one year in arrears shall be declared suspended; *Provided*, said member is not under charges.(a)

565.

22. Lodges shall provide for carrying into effect the beneficial character of the Order, by providing for the payment of weekly benefits in case of disability, and funeral benefits in case of the death of a member; and weekly benefits shall not be less than one dollar per week, nor funeral benefits less than twenty dollars.

OF DELINQUENT OR DEFUNCT LODGES. (b)

566.

SECTION 3. Any Grand or Subordinate Lodge may be suspended or dissolved, and its Charter or Dispensation forfeited to the Supreme or the proper Grand Lodge:

567.

1. For improper conduct.

(a) The proviso to this clause added by the amendment of 1876.

1875, Journal, 1168.
1876, Journal, 1325, 1331.

(b) Original Grand Lodge Constitution.

ARTICLE X.—OF DELINQUENT OR DEFUNCT LODGES.

Sec. 1. Any Lodge may be suspended or dissolved, and its charter or dispensation forfeited to the Grand Lodge.
1. For improper conduct.
2. For neglecting or refusing to conform to the Constitution or Laws of the Grand Lodge, or the general laws and regulations of the Order.
3. For neglecting or refusing to make its returns, or for non-payment of dues to the Grand Lodge. But the charter or dispensation shall not be forfeited in either of the above cases, until the Lodge shall have been duly notified of its offence by the Grand Recording and Corresponding Scribe, and suitable opportunity given them to answer the charges made against it.
4. For neglecting to hold the regular stated meeting as provided by law, unless prevented from doing so by some unforeseen circumstance.
5. By its membership diminishing, so that less than a constitutional quorum may be left.

568.

2. For neglecting or refusing to conform to the Constitution, Laws or Enactments of the Supreme or its Grand Lodge, or the general laws and regulations of the Order.

569.

3. For neglecting or refusing to make its returns, or for non-payment of dues or taxes to the Supreme or its proper Grand Lodge. But the Charter or Dispensation shall not be forfeited in either of the above cases, until the Lodge shall have been duly notified of its offence by the Supreme or proper Grand Keeper of Records and Seal, and suitable opportunity given to answer the charges made against it.

570.

4. For neglecting to hold the regular stated meetings as provided by law, without a proper Dispensation therefor, or unless prevented from doing so by some unforeseen circumstance.

571.

5. By its membership diminishing, so that less than a constitutional quorum may be left.

SEC. 2. When an impeached Lodge neglects or refuses to answer within a given time, it may be tried and suspended for contempt. To suspend a Lodge, requires a two-third vote of all the members present, who may be entitled to vote.

SEC. 3. When a Lodge is suspended or dissolved, it shall be the duty of its last Chancellor Commander, or if there is none, of its senior officer, to deliver up the dipensation or charter, books, jewels, funds, emblems, regalia and other property and effects to the Grand Chancellor or his Deputy, and if any officer or member having custody of any part of the said property or effects, refuses to surrender the same, he may be forever excluded from membership in the Order, even if his Lodge should be reinstated.

SEC. 4. All funds and effects received by the Grand Lodge from a dissolved or suspended Subordinate Lodge, shall be restored in the event of its being reinstated, which reinstatement may be done by the majority vote of the Grand Lodge, at a stated or special session.

SEC. 5. Members of any defunct Lodge, who were in good standing at the time of the dissolution, may be admitted into any other Lodge, after having applied to and received from the Grand Lodge, a card signed by the Grand Chancellor, and countersigned by the Grand Recording and Corresponding Scribe, with the seal of the Grand Lodge attached. The application for such card must be accompanied by the fee of $2; the card to hold good twelve months.

ARTICLE IX. (a)

QUORUM OF VOTES.

572.

A majority of the Grand Lodges shall constitute a quorum to transact business; and a member of a Grand Lodge whose returns for the year and Supreme Representative tax have not been regularly and annually forwarded to the proper Supreme Officers on or before the first day of May (b) prior to any session of the Supreme Lodge, shall in no case be entitled to a vote, either by being an Officer or Supreme Representative.

ARTICLE X. (c)

REVENUE.

573.

Each Grand Lodge shall pay to the Supreme Lodge the sum of $75 dollars annually for each Representative to which they are entitled, and each Grand and Subordinate Lodge shall pay for supplies such sums as may be fixed in the By-Laws of the Supreme Lodge, and all work or supplies so ordered must be paid for when ordering, or on date of delivery.

(a)   Original Supreme Lodge Constitution.

ARTICLE VII.—QUORUM OF VOTES.

A majority of the Grand Lodges shall constitute a quorum to transact business and a member of a Grand Lodge whose returns for the year have not been forwarded to the Supreme Lodge, shall in no case be entitled to a vote, except by unanimous consent.

(b)   Changed from "March" to "May," by amendment of 1876.

1875, Journal, 1169.
1876, Journal, 1326, 1331.

(c)   Original Supreme Lodge Constitution.

ARTICLE VIII.—REVENUE.

SEC. 1.   Each Grand Lodge shall pay to the Supreme Lodge the sum of $75 (2) annually for each Representative they are entitled to.

SEC. 2.   The Charter fees shall be as follows:—For Grand Lodges, $30.   Subordinate Lodges, $15.

SEC. 3.   Grand Lodge Ritual, $3 each, and $15 dollars per set.   Subordinate Lodge Ritual, (to Grand Lodges,) $2 each; $10 per set.   Installation work, (to Grand Lodges,) 25 cents each, $1 per set.·   Odes, (to Grand Lodges,) 2½ cents each, $2.50 per hundred.   Withdrawal Cards, (to Grand Lodges,) 25 cents each.

SEC. 4.   To Subordinate Lodges: Rituals, $4 00 each, $20.00 per set.   Installations, 50 cents each, $2.00 per set.   Odes, 5 cents each, $5.00 per set.

SEC. 5.   All work delivered to Grand and Subordinate Lodges must be paid for within three months after date of delivery.

---

(2)   This Section, until amended in 1871, was " $50," in place of " $75."

1871, Journal, 423.

ARTICLE XI. (a)

MILEAGE.

574.

The Supreme Lodge shall pay the mileage and necessary expenses of its Officers and Representatives to and while in Supreme Session, unless otherwise provided for.

575.

The mileage shall be at the rate of four cents per mile, and four dollars per day during the actual session of the Body.

ARTICLE XII.

REGALIA.

576.

The Regalia of the Supreme, Grand and Subordinate Lodges shall be such as is prescribed by the Supreme Lodge, or adopted and approved from time to time at the Regular Sessions of the Supreme Lodge.

ARTICLE XIII.

CONSTITUTION AND BY-LAWS OBLIGATORY.

577.

All Constitutional provisions contained in all Articles, Sections or paragraphs of this Constitution and By-Laws are obligatory, in every sense, on all Grand and Subordinate Lodges, Knights of Pythias, and all Grand or Subordinate Lodge laws in contravention or conflict herewith are rendered void of effect and illegal in enforcement, or, if enforced, are acts of contumacy, liable and subject to proper punishment.

ARTICLE XIV.

LAWS, WHEN IN FORCE.

578.

All laws, enactments, or legislation of the Supreme Lodge becomes of force from date of passage and publication.

(a) Original Supreme Lodge Constitution.

ARTICLE IX.—MILEAGE.

The Supreme Lodge shall pay the mileage and necessary expenses of its Officers and Representatives.
The mileage shall be at the rate of four (1) cents per mile.

---

(1) This article until amended in 1872 read "six" in place of "four."
1872, Journal, 580, 589, 595.

ARTICLE XV.

SUPREME REPRESENTATIVES' REPORTS.

579.

Supreme Representatives' written reports to their Grand Lodges, or Grand Officers, are official in so far as rendering a Supreme Law operative in its effect prior to the issuance of the Journal of Proceedings or a General Order, and may be recognized until said Journal of Proceedings or General Orders are issued, when said general promulgation and issuance of the Journal or Orders, if differing from their reports in letter, spirit or construction, it (Journal or Orders) must be immediately conformed to in every respect.

ARTICLE XVI.

PASSWORDS.

580.

The Supreme Chancellor shall have exclusive right of creation and promulgation of all passwords proper and fitting for the case involved—to rescind, call in, and change the same, if circumstances require or the exigencies of the case warrant—prescribe their application and use.

ARTICLE XVII.

FOREIGN COUNTRIES.

581.

The Supreme Chancellor may authorize and establish the Order in foreign countries, arrange for and assent to the institution of Grand Lodges therein, under proper reservations for mutual advantage, but, in all instances, exacting and holding intact the spirit, letter and intent, of this Constitution and By-Laws.

ARTICLE XVIII. (a)

ANNUAL RETURNS.

582.

Each Grand Lodge, under the control of the Supreme Lodge, as also all Subordinate Lodges in any State, Country, Island or Territory, where there is no Grand Lodge legally at work or properly instituted, shall make out annual

---

(a) Original Supreme Lodge Constitution.

ARTICLE XI.—DELINQUENT GRAND LODGES.

Any Grand Lodge neglecting to forwards its returns, together with the Representative Tax, due previous to the annual session of the Supreme Lodge, shall disqualify its members from voting in the Supreme Lodge and shall not be entitled to receive the password until said returns and payments are made.

returns of its work and business in accordance with the form sent or delivered to them by the Supreme Keeper of Records and Seal, or other proper officer, and forward the same, with the legal dues or tax from that Body to the Supreme Lodge, to said Supreme Keeper of Records and Seal, on or before the first day of May (a) of each year, or, in default thereof, such Grand Lodge shall forfeit its right to representation at the next session of the Supreme Lodge.

ARTICLE XIX. (b)
APPEALS AND WRITS OF ERROR.

1875, Journal, 1169.
1876, Journal, 1326, 1331.

583.

SECTION 1. All appeals and writs of error, taken from the action or decision of a Grand Lodge or a Subordinate Lodge under the immediate jurisdiction of the Supreme Lodge of the World, to said Supreme Lodge, as hereinafter provided, shall be received and passed upon by said Supreme Lodge, in its capacity of a court of last resort; but in all cases, the action or decision of a Grand Lodge, or a Subordinate Lodge under the immediate jurisdiction of the Supreme Lodge, shall be final and conclusive until reversed by this Supreme Lodge, on appeals or prosecutions of a writ of error therefrom, as hereinafter provided.

584.

SEC. 2. An appeal may be taken from the action or decision of any Subordinate Lodge under the immediate jurisdiction of the Supreme Lodge of the World, to said Supreme Lodge, by any member of such Subordinate Lodge, or by any other person whose rights have been denied by such action or decision, upon giving written notice to said Subordinate Lodge, of said appeal, within two weeks from and after such action or decision.

(a) Changed from " March " to " May " by amendment of 1876.

1875, Journal, 1169.
1876, Journal, 1326, 1331.

(b) This Article in the Constitution as adopted in 1874, and until amended in 1876, read as follows:

"ARTICLE XIV.—APPEALS.

All appeals from the action of Grand or Subordinate Lodges, or by the members thereof, to this Supreme Body, shall be received and passed upon in its capacity of a court of last resort. Said appeals, in proper form, shall come up without any intervention or prevention of Grand or Subordinate Lodges, and when presented for certification by their official seal, the same shall be done."

585.

SEC. 3. With the consent of a Grand Lodge, an appeal may be taken by any Subordinate Lodge, or member under its jurisdiction, from any action or decision of such Grand Lodge, to the Supreme Lodge of the World; *Provided*, however, that such consent shall not be necessary, when a suspended or dissolved Lodge, after having surrendered to its Grand Lodge all its effects, books and property, appeals from such decision; and, provided further, that any action or decision of a Grand Lodge, where is drawn in question any provision of the Constitution, or any enactment or authority of the Supreme Lodge of the World, and the action or decision is against the validity of such provision, enactment or authority, may be examined and reversed or affirmed in the Supreme Lodge of the World, upon a writ of error, to the same extent as could have been done upon an appeal legally taken from such action or decision.

586.

SEC. 4. Such writ of error, as provided for by the last section, may be issued by and upon petition to, either the Grand Chancellor of the Grand Lodge, the action or decision of which is sought to be reviewed, the Supreme Chancellor or the Supreme Lodge of the World, in the case provided for in the last section, and in the order only as above named in this section.

587.

SEC. 5. Consent of a Grand Lodge to appeal must be obtained at the same session at which the action or decision from which such appeal is sought to be taken, was had, and the proper record upon such appeal must be transmitted, properly attested, to the next session of the Supreme Lodge thereafter: provided, that the Supreme Lodge may, in extreme cases, allow the appeal to be entertained at not later than its next following session thereafter. The same rules shall also apply in the prosecution of a writ of error.

588.

SEC. 6. The Supreme Lodge of the World may also adopt such additional rules and regulations as may be deemed necessary and proper to fully carry into effect the foregoing provisions of this article.

ARTICLE XX.

APPLICATION FOR GRAND LODGE CHARTERS.

589.

Grand Lodges working under Dispensation issued by the Supreme Chancellor must apply in regular course, by petition, for their Charter, at the first Regular Session after their institution, which petition shall be accompanied by their Reports, Constitution and By-Laws, all of which shall be referred to the proper Committees, when, the Reports being favorable, and the Committee on Charters and Dispensations reporting and recommending that a Charter be issued, and the Supreme Lodge concurring therein, the Charter shall then be issued, but not otherwise.

ARTICLE XXI.

DEPUTY SUPREME CHANCELLOR.—HONORS.

590.

Any Knight to whom a commission as Deputy Supreme Chancellor shall be issued, in any State, Country, Territory or Island, where the Order is not already established, or if so, where no Grand Lodge exists, shall be entitled to, and receive the Rank of Past Chancellor; and if in a territory where the Order exist, and a Grand Lodge is instituted while he is in charge thereof, he shall be entitled to, and receive at the hands of this Supreme Lodge, the Rank and Grade of Past Grand Chancellor therefor. (a) Except as above, or as otherwise provided in this constitution, the grade or Rank of Past Grand Chancellor shall not be conferred upon any Past Chancellor who has not served as Grand Chancellor; *Provided*, that German District Deputy Grand Chancellors, whose jurisdiction is co-extensive with their State, who have been elected or appointed by the Grand Lodge, and who serve for three successive years, shall be entitled to the Rank of Past Grand Chancellor.

ARTICLE XXII.

DEPUTY SUPREME CHANCELLORS.

591.

All Past Grand or Past Chancellors of *full* Rank regularly authorized and commissioned by the Supreme Chancellor to institute Grand Lodges, or to travel under his instructions to exemplify the Work, shall be known, commissioned and styled Deputy Supreme Chancellors.

(a) The following portion of this article was added by the amendment of 1876.

1875, Journal, 1170.
1876, Journal 1327, 1331.

ARTICLE XXIII.

592.

The necessary expenses incident to traveling to any point and back to original starting point, for the purpose of instituting any Subordinate or Grand Lodge, by the Supreme Chancellor or his Deputy, shall be paid by the Lodges instituted.

ARTICLE XXIV.

RANK CREDENTIALS.

593.

All Knights having Past Rank, removing from one Jurisdiction to another, and desiring to affiliate on a Withdrawal Card, must also present a Rank Credential to entitle him to the same.

ARTICLE XXV.

BALLOT—BLACK BALLS.

594.

Grand Lodges may legislate in their local law to prescribe that one black ball may reject, in cases of application for membership, but shall not increase the same to more than as prescribed in the Supreme Maximum of *two*.

ARTICLE XXVI.

SEALS.

595.

All Grand and Subordinate Lodges shall have an appropriate Seal bearing proper devices thereon, name, number and location of the Lodge, with the date of its institution thereon, a good copy or impression of which shall be deposited with the Supreme Keeper of Records and Seal.

ARTICLE XXVII.

COMPILED PROCEEDINGS.

596.

It shall be obligatory on all Grand and Subordinate Lodges of this Order, to have a full volume of Supreme Lodge proceedings and Laws as issued, on hand for ready reference on law or usage points; and hereafter for any and all new Subordinate Lodges, one full copy or set of Supreme Lodge Proceedings shall constitute an indispensable part of their supplies to be sent out and paid for. All "sets" of Work, etc., as herein enumerated, shall constitute the legal number to be issued by any and all Grand Lodges or Officers, which shall neither be added to or taken from by them, and all Work delivered to Grand and Subordinate Lodges or Officers ordering the same, must be paid for on date of delivery, free of expense to the Supreme Lodge.

ARTICLE XXVIII. (a)
ELECTIONS—SUPREME LODGE.
597.

The Supreme Lodge Officers shall be elected bi-annually by ballot. A majority of all the votes present shall be necessary to constitute a choice. In case of a tie, the balloting shall continue until a choice is made; the name of the Brother receiving the lowest number of votes at each balloting shall be withdrawn. Any Officer who may be absent at the time of installation, unless excused by the Supreme Lodge, or by sickness, his office shall be declared vacant, and another and immediate election held to fill the vacancy. But if the absent Officer elect has been excused, or is ill, then the Supreme Chancellor may be empowered to install during recess, at his convenience.

ARTICLE XXIX. (b)
TRAVELING SHIELDS.
598.

Traveling Shields, for the use of Brethren, can only be used or recognized when procured from the Supreme Lodge, and are of the prescribed and legal form, as adopted, and under its restrictions as made for general or special use, by Grand Lodges, and from them issued to the Subordinate Lodges for issuance to members, *except* it be where no Grand Lodge is in existence, or recognized by this Supreme Lodge, and in such cases from the Deputy Supreme Chancellor in charge of said State or Territory.

(a) Original Supreme Lodge Constitution:
ARTICLE X.
ELECTION OF SUPREME LODGE OFFICERS.

SECTION 1. The Supreme Lodge Officers shall be elected bi-annually; the first election after the adoption of this Constitution occurring on the second Tuesday in March, A. D. 1870.

SEC. 2. The Supreme Lodge Officers shall be elected by ballot. A majority of all the votes present shall be necessary to constitute a choice. In case of a tie, the balloting shall continue until a choice is made; the name of the brother receiving the lowest number of votes at each balloting shall be withdrawn.

(b) Original Supreme Lodge Constitution:
ARTICLE XV. (1)

No visiting cards shall be used in the Order.

---

(1) ARTICLE XVII of Grand Lodge Constitution was exactly the same as this.

ARTICLE XXX.

UNIFORM AND REGALIA.

599.

All Supreme, Grand or Subordinate Lodge Officers appearing in the prescribed uniform of the Order indicative of their rank, and wearing the proper and prescribed official Jewel on their left breast; or,

600.

All Past Supreme, Grand or Subordinate Lodge Officers appearing appareled in a like manner, wearing the proper and prescribed Past Official Jewel on their left breast; or,

601.

Any and all Knights appearing and appareled in a like manner, with the Knight's Jewel on his left breast, shall be considered in full and complete regalia for all Lodge Conventions, meetings or session purposes, being entitled to admission to, and seat within any Lodge of the Order (if otherwise qualified and entitled to admission) wherever existing. But in the absence of the uniform, the Jewel alone shall not be considered sufficient regalia, except for officers of Subordinate Lodges in their Conventions and at their stations; and the following shall be the Regalia, when used, of the several Bodies as below, to-wit:

(a) The Regalia of the Supreme Lodge shall be as follows:

602.

For Past Supreme Chancellor—A purple collar, skirted with scarlet and white, the scarlet to be inside; to be trimmed with helmet, globe and tassels, lace and fringe of gilt bullion. Jewel, of white and yellow metals, to be worn pendant thereto, with the words Past Supreme Chancellor, enameled or engraved on the border.

(a) Original Supreme Lodge Constitution:

ARTICLE XII.—REGALIA.

The Regalia of the Supreme Lodge shall be as follows:

For Founder and Past Supreme Chancellor, a purple collar, skirted with scarlet and white; the scarlet to be inside, to be trimmed with helmet, globe and tassels, lace, and fringe of gilt bullion. Jewel—Knight's mark or coat of arms, with the words, "Founder of the Order K. of P." engraved on the border.

For Past Supreme Chancellors—The same collar and Jewel, but upon the latter "Past Supreme Chancellor," on the circle or oval surrounding the helmet, instead of "Founder," etc.

For Supreme Venerable Patriarch — White collar, skirted with scarlet, trimmed with gilt lace and bullion fringe and tassels. On the right breast of the collar shall be embroidered in gilt bullion, a visored helmet, with axe and lance crossed, illustrative of the name

603.

For Supreme Chancellor and Supreme Vice Chancellor—
Collars of purple, skirted with scarlet, of the same form,
style and trimming (including helmet and globe) as the
sitting Past Supreme Chancellor. Jewels to be of yellow
and white metals, as provided and adopted, of the same
device in emblems, unless otherwise specifically stated, as
those worn by the corresponding officers of Grand and
Subordinate Lodges, and to be worn suspended from the
collar, in the same manner as above stated, or used in
prescribed manner for them.

604.

For remaining Supreme Officers—Same as specified for
Supreme Chancellor.

605.

For Supreme Prelate—White collar, skirted with scarlet,
trimmed with gilt lace and bullion fringe and tassels. On
the right breast of the collar shall be embroidered in gilt
bullion a visored helmet, with axe and lance crossed, illustrative of the name and general character of the Order.
On the left breast shall be embroidered in gilt bullion a
globe, emblematical of universal fraternity, and the supreme
authority of this Lodge. The Jewel, of white and yellow
metals, shall be as prescribed and adopted, to be worn suspended from the collar where the ends are united, or suspended on the left breast in open sight if in uniform and
detached from Regalia.

606.

For Supreme Representatives—The same as P.G.C's, with
"S.R." upon the right-hand side of collar, in gilt bullion,
with Jewel pendant, or as otherwise prescribed for members
in uniform.

---

and general character of the Order. On the left breast shall be
embroidered in gilt bullion a globe, emblematical of universal fraternity, and the supreme authority of this Lodge. The Jewel shall be
an open Bible of yellow metal, and to be worn suspended from the
collar where the ends are united.

For Supreme Chancellor and remaining officers, shall wear collars
of purple, skirted with scarlet, of the same form, style and trimming
(including helmet and globe) as the Supreme Venerable Patriarch.
Jewels to be of yellow metal, of the same device as those worn by the
corresponding officers of Grand and Subordinate Lodges, and to be
worn suspended from the collar, in the same manner as above stated.

For P.G.C's., black collar, trimmed with gilt lace, and fringe.

For Supreme Representatives, the same, with "S.R." upon the
collar, in gilt bullion.

No member shall be allowed to enter the Supreme Lodge when in
session, unless clothed in the established Regalia of his rank.

607.

No Past Officer, Representative, or member, shall be allowed to enter the Supreme Lodge when in session, unless properly uniformed and jeweled, or clothed in the established regalia of his Rank, according to these prescriptions, with Jewel appended thereto; *Provided*, Any Past Chancellor, officer, or member presenting himself at the door of any Lodge of the Order properly uniformed, as prescribed by the Supreme Lodge law, with the Past Official, Official, or Knight's Jewel on his left breast, in open sight, shall be recognized as in proper regalia, and be entitled to admittance, if otherwise qualified.

(a) The working Regalia of Grand Lodges shall be as follows, to wit:

608.

P. G. Chancellors—Black velvet collar, trimmed with gold lace and fringe, and P.G.C. embroidered in gold on left side, with the approved and adopted Jewel pendant.

609.

Past Chancellors—Red velvet collar, trimmed with gold fringe, and adopted and approved Jewel pendant.

(a) Original Grand Lodge Constitution:

ARTICLE VIII.—REGALIA. (1)

The working regalia shall be as follows:
V.G.P.—Black velvet collar, trimmed with gold fringe, and open Bible in gold on left side.
P.G. Chancellors—Black velvet collar trimmed with gold fringe, with P.G.C. embroidered in gold on left side.
P. Chancellors—Red velvet collar, trimmed with gold fringe.
Representatives—Same as Past Chancellors, rosette with number of Lodge on left side. Said rosette to be furnished by the Subordinate Lodge represented.
Officers—Same as Past Chancellors, with the insignia of office embroidered in gold on left side.

---

(1) This Article until 1871 had another section which was at that time repealed; the section being as follows:
"SEC. 2. The established outside regalia, if used, shall be as follows:
For G C.—An apron made of the best silk velvet, with lappel, and upon lappel letters K.P., crossed lances and helmet, with letter F.C.B. arched over it, and letters P.C on either side of the apron—the whole apron to be fringed with silver one and a half inches in length, and all letters and emblems to be embroidered in silver. In addition, a black rosette of ribbon work upon the lappel of the coat, on the rosette crossed gavels in white metal, moveable. On the outer edge of the apron, adjoining the fringe, will be placed a red velvet border, adjoining that a border of gold, then a border of blue velvet.
For V.G.C.—Same as G.C., except on rosette but one gavel.
For V.G.P.—Same as G.C., on rosette open Bible.
For G.R S —Same as G.C., on rosette crossed pens.
For G.B.--Same as G.C., on rosette crossed keys.
For G.G.—Same as G.C., on rosette staffs crossed.
For G.I.S.—Same as G.C., on rosette crossed swords.
For G O S.—Same as G.C., on rosette one sword.
For Representative.—Same as G.C., on rosette letter R.
For P.C.—Same as G.C., no rosette.
For Deputy Grand Chancellor, the working regalia shall be a red velvet collar trimmed with gold fringe, and the letter D.G.C. embroidered thereon in gold. The apron regalia of the D.G.C. shall be the same as a Past Chancellor's regalia. He shall also wear a rosette with D.G.C. upon it."

1871, Journal, 362, 384, 412.

610.

Representatives—Same as Past Chancellors, rosette with number of Lodge on left side, and approved and adopted Jewel pendant. Said rosette to be furnished by the Subordinate Lodge represented.

611.

Officers—Same as Past Chancellors, with the prescribed insignia of office of their Rank, adopted and approved Jewel pendant; *Provided*, Any officer, Representative, or Past Chancellor, presenting himself properly uniformed, as prescribed by the Supreme Lodge Law, with the Past Official or Official Jewel on his left breast, in open sight, shall be recognized as in proper regalia, and be entitled to admittance, if otherwise qualified.

612.

(a) The working Regalia of Subordinate Lodges shall be as follows, to-wit:

For Pages a blue collar; for Esquires, a yellow collar; for Knights, a red collar. Officers' Regalia—For C.C., a collar of scarlet velvet, with silver fringe 1½ inches long, and silver lace border on inner edge half inch wide, with Jewel pendant: for V.C., the same as the C.C., with Jewel pendant; for Prelate, a black velvet collar, trimmed same as C.C. and

---

(a) Original Subordinate Lodge Constitution:

ARTICLE XI.—REGALIA. (1)

The working regalia shall be as follows: For Pages, a blue collar; for Esquires, a yellow collar; for Knights, a red collar; for Prelate, a black velvet collar, with silver fringe 1½ inches long, and silver lace border on inner edge half inch wide, and an open bible embroidered in silver on the left side; for C.C. a collar of scarlet velvet, trimmed in same manner as the Prelate's, with crossed gavels on left side; for V.C. the same as the C.C.'s., with single gavel; for K. of R. and S. the same as the V.C.'s with crossed pens, omitting the fringe; for M. of F. the same as the K. of R. and S. with pen and key crossed; for M of E. the same as the M. of F.'s., with crossed keys; for M. at A. the same as the M. of E. with crossed staffs; for I.G. the same as the M. at A., with crossed swords; for O.G. the same as the I.G. with single sword; for P.C. the same as the C.C.'s., with gold fringe and without the gavels.

---

(1) This Article until 1872, had another section which was Sec. 1, and was repealed at that time. This Section read as follows:

SEC. 1. The regalia for Subordinate Lodges, if used, shall be as follows:

For Pages, a black and white apron, made of the best merino, fifteen inches in length in middle, and sixteen inches in width; lappel to be six inches and a half in length from top to end of point, with the letters K.P. embroidered on it in silver; on apron crossed lances embroidered in silver, with the letter "F." embroidered in blue, silver fringe around the apron one and a half inches in length; Euing to be black muslin, strings black, lances to be five inches in length.

For Esquires the same as Page, with an additional letter "C." embroidered in gold.

For Knights, the same as Esquire, with an addition letter "B" embroidered in red.

For officers, the same as Knights, with a rosette of black and white ribbon, white on outer edge, also the insignia of office in centre of rosette, made out of white metal and movable. The rosette to be worn on lappel of coat on left side. The V.P., R.S. and B. of Lodge wear the P.C. apron, with rosette, as above.

and V.C., with Jewel pendant; for M. of E., the same as the V.C., omitting the fringe, with Jewel pendant; for M. of F., the same as the M. of E., with Jewel pendant; for K. of R. and S., the same as the M. of F., with Jewel pendant; for M. at A., the same as the K. of R. and S., with Jewel pendant; for I. G., the same as the M. at A., with Jewel pendant; for O. G., the same as the I. G., with Jewel pendant; for P.C., the same as the C. C., with gold fringe, with Jewel pendant; or, in other words, plain collars, the same as the above in every particular, *except* the embroidered emblems as heretofore used, and in their place the adopted metal jewels hanging pendant thereto; *Provided*, that any and all Lodges of this Order, wherever hereafter started, on and after July 1, 1874, shall procure and use only the plain Regalia and prescribed metal Jewels (if desiring both) or Jewels alone; that any and all Lodges now having and using the Regalia *with* the "embroidered emblems" *on* them, may do so until worn out, but when replacing them, either in part or whole, shall conform strictly to the provisions as herein expressed and above set forth; conditioned that no part of this provision shall be so construed by any authority to prevent Lodge Officers, when working, using the Jewels alone, without any Regalia, or any Lodge now having and using the style of Regalia with embroidered emblems thereon, from using the metal Jewel in connection therewith; *Provided*, any Past Chancellor, officer, or member, presenting himself properly uniformed, as prescribed by the Supreme Lodge Law, with the Past Official, Official, or Knight's Jewel on his left breast, in open sight, shall be recognized in proper Regalia, and be entitled to admittance, if otherwise qualified; (a) *Provided, however*, any Past Supreme Officer, Supreme Officer, Supreme Representative, Past Supreme Representative, Past Grand Officer, Grand Officer, Past Chancellor and Subordinate Lodge Officer, and Knight wearing the Jewel of his Rank on the left lappel of the coat in a Lodge, shall be considered in full regalia.

ARTICLE XXXI.
SUSPENSION OF LODGES.
613.

The Supreme and each Grand Lodge may provide for and order the revocation of any or all Dispensations or Charters and suspension of Subordinate Lodges under their Jurisdiction for violations of this Constitution, Supreme Lodge orders, enactments, legislation or decisions, or their Grand

---

(a) This proviso was added by the amendment of 1876.
1875, Journal, 1170.
1876, Journal, 1328, 1331.

Lodge constitutional provisions, local laws, or Grand Chancellor's official mandates during recess.

ARTICLE XXXII. (a)
TERMS.
614.

A term of the Supreme Lodge shall be two years, and the term of Subordinate Lodges, working immediately under the control of the Supreme Lodge shall be six months, and the terms of Grand Lodges shall be one year, and that the terms of Subordinate Lodges, working under the control of Grand Lodges shall be remitted to the several Grand Jurisdictions; *Provided*, that no term of a Subordinate Lodge shall be less than six months.

ARTICLE XXXIII. (b)
AMENDMENTS.
615.

No alteration or amendment to the Constitution of the Supreme Lodge shall be made unless presented at a Regular Session, and adopted by a two-thirds vote, at the next succeeding Regular Session; *Provided*, that no change shall be made in the Written or Unwritten Work unless the same lay over from one Session to another, nor then, unless four-fifths of the Representatives concur therein.

(a) This Article inserted entire by the amendment of 1876. See note, Article XXXIII.

1875, Journal, 1171.
1876, Journal, 1328, 1331.

(b) This, in the Constitution of 1874, was numbered XXXII, but was changed in 1876.

1875, Journal, 1171.
1876, Journal, 1328, 1331.

The original in Supreme Lodge Constitution was, as follows:

ARTICLE XIII.—AMENDMENTS. (1)

No alteration or amendment to the Constitution of the Supreme, Grand or Subordinate Lodges shall be made, unless presented in writing, specifying the article, section and line intended to be amended, at an Annual Session, and adopted by a two-third vote at the next succeeding regular session.

---

(1) This Article originally, had not the words " at the next succeeding regular session " at the end ; nor the words "in writing, specifying the article, section and line intended to be amended," the former having been added in 1872, and the latter in 1873.

1872, Journal, 592, 596, 623, 642.
1873, Journal, 751.

BY-LAWS.

1874, Journal, 946, 947, 966, 967.

616.

All printed or other materials furnished by the Supreme Lodge to any Grand or Subordinate Lodge, members thereof, or other parties, for creating a revenue for the Supreme Lodge, shall be known under the general heading of "Supplies," which said supplies shall be furnished as may be from time to time specified, changed, altered or amended by legislation at the Regular Sessions, but which for the time being shall be as follows, to-wit:

617. Supplies to Grand Lodges.

Dispensation Fee to Grand Lodges	$30 00
Charter Fee	20 00
Charter Plates for Subordinates	2 00
Grand Lodge Rituals, $5 each, per set of 5	25 00
Rituals for Subordinate Lodges, each	2 00
Installation Books for Subordinate Lodges, each	40
Odes for Subordinate Lodges, each	5
Odes for Grand Lodges, each	10
Bound Journals of Proceedings of Supreme Lodge, in paper	1 00
Compiled Proceedings of Supreme Lodge, in leather,	5 00
Odes of the Order, set to Music, per book	20
Dedication Ceremonies, per book, $1 each, per set	5 00
Traveling Shields	20
Withdrawal Cards	25

618. Supplies to Subordinate Lodges under the immediate Jurisdiction of the Supreme Lodge.

Dispensation Fee	$15 00
Rituals, per set of 5	20 00
Installation, per set of 5	3 00
Odes, 10 cents each, per set of 50	5 00
Bound Journals of Supreme Lodge Proceedings, in paper	1 00
Compiled Proceedings, in leather	5 00
Odes of the Order, set to Music, 40 cents per book; per set of 5	2 00
Traveling Shields	40
Withdrawal Cards	50

OFFICIAL JEWELS FOR SUPREME, GRAND, AND SUBORDINATE LODGES, PAST OFFICERS AND KNIGHTS.

1873, Journal, 701, 702.
1874, Journal, 973–979.
1875, Journal, 1026, 1135.

[The illustrations on pages 138 and 139 are for Subordinate Lodge; page 140, Past Grand Chancellor, Past Chancellor and Knight, and are nearly half size of the Jewels.]

619. Grand Lodge Jewels.

No. 1. Set of 11 Jewels, including two for Supreme Representatives..$40 00
Triangle, German silver, heavily plated with silver. Oval of Oreide, heavily gilt, and neatly engraved.

No. 2. Set of 11 Jewels 55 00
Triangle and Emblems coin silver, solid. Shield and Oval of Oreide, very heavily gilt. More elaborate engraving and chased.

620. Subordinate Lodge Jewels

No. 3. Set of 14 Jewels, including four for attendants 18 00
Triangle and White Emblems, of German silver, well silver-plated, neatly engraved, and burnished on front. Colored Emblems, of gilt.

No. 4. Set of 14 Jewels 25 00
Triangle and White Emblems, of German silver, triple plated, burnished both sides, more elaborate engraving. Colored Emblems, solid, heavily gilt and chased.

No. 5. Set of 14 Jewels.. 45 00
Triangle and White Emblems, of coin silver, burnished both sides, very elaborate engraving. Colored Emblems, solid, very heavily gilt and chased.

621. Past Chancellor's Jewels—Separate from Sets.

No. 6. Same quality as No. 3. Price............ .....$1 80 each.
" 7.   "   "   " 4.   " .... 2 80   "
" 8.   "   "   " 5.   " .... 5 00   "

622. Past Grand Chancellors' and District Deputy G. C.'s Jewels.

No. 9. Same quality as No. 1. Price.............$4 50 each.
" 10.   "   "   " 2.   " .... 5 50   "

623. Knight's Jewels.

No. 11. Same quality as No. 3. Price.............$2 20 each.
" 12.   "   "   " 4.   " .... 3 25   "
" 13.   "   "   " 5.   " .... 5 00   "

If ten or more Knights' Jewels are ordered at one time, ten per cent. will be deducted from above prices.

624.

All Jewels will have a neat Pin, from which the Jewel will be pendant.

C. C.

V. C.

Prelate.

M. of E.

M. of F.

K. of R. and S.

M. at A.

I. G.

O. G.

Attendant.

P. G. C.

P. C.

Knight.

MEMORIAL CHARTS.

1874, Journal, 904, 979–983, 989.
1875, Journal, 1023, 1126.

625. Form A—Knight's Chart.
Black and tinted border, lettering in centre, blue, $1 50 each.
In lots of 100 or more.. 80 "
   "   75.. 85 "
   "   50.. 90 "
   "   25.. 95 "
   "   10.. 1 00 "
Less than 10 at one order, at retail price.

626. Form B—Past Chancellor's Chart.
Black and tinted border, lettering in centre, green, $1 75 each.
In lots of 50 or more.. 90 "
   "   25.. 95 "
   "   10.. 1 00 "
   "   5.. 1 10 "
Less than 5 at one order, at retail price.

627. Form C—Past Grand Chancellor's Chart.
Black and tinted border, lettering in centre, red, $2 00 each.
In lots of 20 or more.. 1 00 "
   "   10.. 1 10 "
   "   5.. 1 25 "
Less than 5 at one order, at retail price.

OFFICIAL RECEIPT.

627a. Resolutions establishing.
Resolved, That the Supreme Chancellor and the Supreme Keeper of Records and Seal be, and hereby are, authorized to issue receipts which shall be furnished to all Grand and Subordinate Lodges at $2.00 per 100; and that no receipt shall be authoritative or evidence of payment of dues, assessments or other claims of the Lodge, unless written upon such receipt, and bearing the seal of the Supreme Lodge.

Resolved, That the receipt above mentioned, go into effect on and after July 1st, 1875.

1875, Journal, 1165.

RULES OF ORDER.

1874, Journal, 990.
1875, Journal, 1095, 1098, 1108-1111.

628.

1. The presiding officer having taken the chair, the officers and members shall take their respective seats, and at the sound of the gavel there shall be a general silence.

629.

2. At the appointed hour the Supreme Chancellor shall organize the meeting, by directing the Supreme Keeper of Records and Seal to call the names of the Officers of this Supreme Lodge. After which he shall make report of the number of Grand Lodges from which Representatives are present; when, if a quorum be present, the Supreme Chancellor shall call on the Supreme Prelate to address the Supreme Ruler of the Universe in prayer. The Supreme Vice Chancellor and the Supreme Master-at-Arms shall then examine the Representatives present, and report to the Supreme Chancellor, and, if correct, the Supreme Chancellor shall direct the members to clothe themselves with their regalia and take their seats, after which the Supreme Vice Chancellor, at the request of the Supreme Chancellor, shall proclaim the Lodge duly opened.

630.

3. The business shall be taken up in the following order: The Supreme Lodge shall be opened in due form.

631.

4. The Supreme Keeper of Records and Seal will report on the certificates of Representatives, which shall be referred to the proper committee.

632.

5. The Supreme Chancellor shall appoint a Committee on Credentials and Returns, and a Committee on Allotment of Seats—each committee to consist of five* members. Both of said committees shall report without delay, and said reports shall be acted upon and disposed of before any other business is transacted.

633.

6. On the adoption of . the report of the Committee on Credentials and Returns, recommending the admission of the Past Grand Chancellors and Representatives, they shall be admitted in form.

---

*1876, Journal, 1325, 1329, 1332.

634.

7. The minutes of the last annual and intervening meetings shall be read and passed upon.

635.

8. The report of the Supreme Chancellor as to his acts and doings during the recess of the Supreme Lodge, shall be presented.

636.

9. The annual reports of the Supreme Keeper of Records and Seal, and Supreme Master of Exchequer, shall be presented.

637.

10. The Supreme Chancellor shall then appoint the following committees, each to consist of five* members, viz:

Committee on Law and Supervision.
Committee on Finance.
Committee on Appeals and Grievances.
Committee on Mileage.
Committee on State of the Order.
Committee on Written Work.
Committee on Unwritten Work.
Committee on Printing.
Committee on Dispensations and Charters.

638.

11. The Jurisdictions shall be called in their order of seniority, when any legitimate business may be presented.

639.

12. Petitions shall be presented, read and referred.

640.

13. Reports of Standing Committees to be called by the Supreme Chancellor in the order of their appointment.

641.

14. Reports of Special Committees.

642.

15. Miscellaneous Business.

---

*1876, Journal, 1325, 1329, 1332.

11

643.

16. The above order of business may be transposed or dispensed with, at the discretion of the Supreme Lodge. When the business of the session is concluded, the Supreme Prelate shall offer a prayer, and the Supreme Vice Chancellor shall proclaim the Supreme Lodge duly closed.

644.

17. Voting for officers shall be by ballot. All other voting shall be *viva voce*, or by yeas and nays, as the Supreme Lodge may determine.

645.

18. On the call of two Jurisdictions, the yeas and nays shall be taken on any question, and when taken shall be entered on the journal.

646.

19. No motion shall be subject to debate until it has been seconded and stated by the chair. It shall be reduced to writing at the request of any member.

647.

20. When a question is before the Supreme Lodge, no motion shall be received, unless it be to adjourn, the previous question, to lie on the table, to refer, to postpone indefinitely, to postpone to a certain time, to recommit, or to amend; and the motions just enumerated shall take precedence in the order of enumeration. The first three shall be decided without debate.

648.

21. When a subject has been indefinitely postponed, it cannot again, during the same session, be taken up and considered; nor can a subject which the Supreme Lodge has refused to reconsider, be taken up at that session.

649.

22. On a call of representatives of three Grand Jurisdictions, a majority of the Supreme Lodge may demand that the previous question shall be put, which shall always be in this form: "*Shall the main question be now put?*" and, until it is decided, no further debate shall take place, and the vote shall be taken, first, on any amendments that may be pending, and next on the final question.

650.

23. When the reading of any paper or other matter is called for, and the same is objected to by any member, it shall be determined by vote of the Supreme Lodge without debate.

651.

24. Before putting a question, the presiding officer shall ask, "*Is the Supreme Lodge ready for the question?*" If no member rise to speak, and a majority of the Supreme Lodge are ready for the question, he shall rise and put it. While the presiding officer is putting a question, or addressing the Supreme Lodge, none shall walk out of or across the room, nor entertain private discourse; and after he shall have risen to put it, no member shall speak upon it.

652.

25. The presiding officer, or any other member doubting the decision of a question, may call for a division of the Supreme Lodge; but a division cannot be called for after the Chair has announced the result of a vote.

653.

26. No member shall be permitted to speak or vote unless clothed in regalia according to his rank and station, and occupying his seat at the place designated for him.

654.

27. During the progress of a ballot for an officer, no motion can be entertained, or debate or explanation permitted.

655.

28. Every officer and member shall be designated by his proper title or office according in the Order.

656.

29. Every member, when he speaks or offers a motion, shall rise and respectfully address and be recognized by the presiding officer; and while speaking he shall confine himself to the question in debate, avoiding all personalities and indecorous language, as well as all reflections upon the the Supreme Lodge or any of its members.

657.

30. Should two or more members rise to speak at the same time, the Chair shall decide which is entitled to the floor; and no member shall interrupt or disturb another while speaking, unless to call him to order for words spoken.

658.

31. If a member, while speaking, shall be called to order, he shall, at the request of the Chair, take his seat until the question of order is determined, when he may proceed again.

659.

32. The decisions of the Chair on points of order, may be appealed from by any member, which point of order shall be reduced to writing; and in such cases the question shall be, "*Shall the decision of the Chair stand as the judgment of the Supreme Lodge?*"

660.

33. No member shall speak more than once on the same question, until all the members wishing to speak have had an opportunity to do so; and no one shall speak more than ten minutes on any question, unless by permission of the Supreme Lodge.

661.

34. When a petition, memorial, or communication is presented, a brief statement of its contents shall be made by the introducer or the Chair; and, after it has been read, a brief notice of its purport shall be entered upon the journal.

662.

35. When a blank is to be filled, the question shall be taken first upon the highest sum or number, and the longest or latest time proposed.

663.

36. Any member may call for a division of a question, when the sense will admit.

664.

37. After any question, except one of indefinite postponement, or one which the Supreme Lodge has refused to reconsider, has been decided, any two members who voted in the majority, may, at the same or next session, move for a reconsideration thereof; but no discussion of the main question shall be allowed until reconsidered.

665.

38. No matter shall be considered at any morning session of the Supreme Lodge, until all the committees shall have had an opportunity of presenting reports.

666.

39. A committee appointed at one session to perform a duty, are bound to report, although some of the members of the committee have ceased to be members of this body.

667.

40. Any member has a right to protest, and to have an epitome of his protest spread upon the journal, if in respectful language.

668.

41. Every member is bound to vote, serve on committees, and accept nominations, unless excused by vote.

669.

42. No member shall be allowed to cast his vote after a ballot has been announced.

670.

43. No more than two amendments to a proposition shall be entertained at the same time; that is, an amendment, and an amendment to an amendment, and the question shall be first taken on the latter.

671.

44. Any proposition offered for reference to any Standing or Special Committee of this body, which shall require an entry in full upon the journal, shall be submitted in duplicate, either in print or in manuscript; and if in writing, they shall be on paper not less in size than half a page of foolscap. All resolutions and legislative measures belonging to or within the purview of any standing or special committee of this body, shall be referred in the regular order to said committees, before reported on and submitted by them for action thereon, by the Supreme Lodge.

672.

45. The Supreme Chancellor shall appoint a Standing Committee on Rules, to whom shall be referred all amendments thereto, and all questions of order not otherwise disposed of.

673.

46. The election of officers shall take place on such day of the session as the Supreme Lodge may determine.

674.

47. The installation of officers shall be after the business of the session, at which the election takes place, has been completed.

675.

48. Cushing's Manual (a) shall be our standard for parliamentary law, in the absence of any rule governing our action.

676.

49. Proposals to add to, amend or alter these Rules, shall be submitted in writing and lay over at least one day, when a majority vote shall adopt or reject.

(a) Original Supreme Lodge Constitution.

ARTICLE XIV.—RULES OF ORDER.

☞ "Cushing's Manual" shall govern the parliamentary practice of this Supreme Lodge.

ANALYTICAL INDEX.

AUTHORITY:

156 ANALYTICAL INDEX.

CUSHING'S MANUAL: Sections.
the standard, for parliamentary law 675

DANISH:
Ritual authorized to be translated into 342

DEDICATIONS:
public, provided for 39

DEMANDS:
only evidence of payment of 265, 266, 269

DEGREES:
this title replaced by Ranks 322

DEPUTY GRAND CHANCELLOR:
may communicate P.W. to C.C., outside of Lodge Room..280, 471
may give secret work outside of Lodge Room 471
German, when entitled to honors of P.G.C.. 590

DEPUTY SUPREME CHANCELLOR:
commission to 50, 360
has no authority to charter new Lodge.................. 51
to report moneys sent Supreme Lodge..............35, 38
to approve or disapprove petitions for new Lodges, when..185, 186
how appointed and commissioned 510
duties of...510, 516
may institute Grand Lodge and install officers of......510, 535
also install officers of Subordinate Lodges, when........ 516
when entitled to honors of P.C. and when to P.G.C........ 590
how title of, acquired................................. 591

DIAGRAMS:
work in Book of, how changed 470
Book of, prepared by Supreme Lodge 472

DISCIPLINE:
of the Order, to be uniform 504

DISPENSATIONS:
cannot issue, by Deputy S. C. for new Lodge.......... 51
cannot issue, to initiate for less than legal fees......63, 84
may issue by Grand Lodge to initiate maimed person...... 89, 220
may issue by Grand Chancellor to initiate maimed person, 83, 221
may issue by Supreme Chancellor to initiate maimed person, 222
to be issued as of the proper Pythian Period......... 317, 318
for new Lodges, when issued by Supreme Chancellor 507, 508
how long to remain in force........................... 507
list of, for Charters, etc., to be kept by S. K. of R. and S......... 514

170   ANALYTICAL INDEX.

  13

www.ingramcontent.com/pod-product-compliance
Lightning Source LLC
Chambersburg PA
CBHW030537040726
47497CB00008B/2486